D0651581

HORSES AND MEN

¶ A descriptive list of some of the volumes in THE TRAVELLERS' LIBRARY will be found at the end of the volume.

¶ As further volumes are constantly being added to the Library, it is not always possible to keep these lists fully up to date. For the latest lists application should be made to any bookseller, or to the publishers.

HORSES AND MEN

by

SHERWOOD ANDERSON

NEW YORK

JONATHAN CAPE AND HARRISON SMITH

FIRST ISSUED IN THE TRAVELLERS' LIBRARY 1929

CONTENTS

TO
THEODORE DREISER
IN WHOSE PRESENCE I HAVE SOMETIMES HAD
THE SAME REFRESHED FEELING AS WHEN IN
THE PRESENCE OF A THOROUGHBRED HORSE

DID you ever have a notion of this kind? – there is an orange, or say an apple, lying on a table before you. You put out your hand to take it. Perhaps you eat it, make it a part of your physical life. Have you touched? Have you eaten? That's what I wonder about.

The whole subject is only important to me because I want the apple. What subtle flavours are concealed in it – how does it taste, smell, feel? Heavens, man, the way the apple feels in the hand is something – isn't it?

For a long time I thought only of eating the apple. Then later its fragrance became something of importance, too. The fragrance stole out through my room, through a window and into the streets. It made itself a part of all the smells of the streets. The devil! – in Chicago or Pittsburg, Youngstown or Cleveland it would have had a rough time.

That doesn't matter.

The point is that after the form of the apple began to take my eye I often found myself unable to touch at all. My hands went toward the object of my desire and then came back.

There I sat, in the room with the apple before me, and hours passed. I had pushed myself off into a world where nothing has any existence. Had I done that, or had I merely stepped, for the moment, out of the world of darkness into the light?

It may be that my eyes are blind and that I cannot see. It may be I am deaf.

My hands are nervous and tremble. How much do they tremble? Now, alas! I am absorbed in looking at my own hands.

With these nervous and uncertain hands may I really feel for the form of things concealed in the darkness?

DREISER

Heavy, heavy, hangs over thy head,
Fine, or superfine?

THEODORE DREISER is old — he is very, very old. I do not know how many years he has lived, perhaps forty, perhaps fifty, but he is very old. Something grey and bleak and hurtful, that has been in the world perhaps for ever, is personified in him.

When Dreiser is gone men shall write books, many of them, and in the books they shall write there will be so many of the qualities Dreiser lacks. The new, the younger men shall have a sense of humour, and everyone knows Dreiser has no sense of humour. More than that, American prose writers shall have grace, lightness of touch, a dream of beauty breaking through the husks of life.

Oh, those who follow him shall have many things that Dreiser does not have! That is a part of the wonder and beauty of Theodore Dreiser, the things that others shall have, because of him.

Long ago, when he was editor of the *Delineator*, Dreiser went one day, with a woman friend, to visit an orphan asylum. The woman once told me the story of that afternoon in the big, ugly grey building, with Dreiser, looking heavy and lumpy and old, sitting on a platform, folding and refolding his pocket-handkerchief and watching the children — all in their little uniforms, trooping in.

'The tears ran down his cheeks and he shook his head,' the woman said, and that is a real picture of Theodore Dreiser. He is old in spirit and he does not know what to do with life, so he tells about it as he sees it, simply and honestly. The tears run down his cheeks and he folds and refolds the pocket-handkerchief and shakes his head.

11

Heavy, heavy, the feet of Theodore. How easy to pick some of his books to pieces, to laugh at him for so much of his heavy prose.

The feet of Theodore are making a path, the heavy brutal feet. They are tramping through the wilderness of lies, making a path. Presently the path will be a street, with great arches overhead and delicately carved spires piercing the sky. Along the street will run children, shouting, 'Look at me. See what I and my fellows of the new day have done' – forgetting the heavy feet of Dreiser.

The fellows of the ink-pots, the prose writers in America who follow Dreiser, will have much to do that he has never done. Their road is long but, because of him, those who follow will never have to face the road through the wilderness of Puritan denial, the road that Dreiser faced alone.

> *Heavy, heavy, hangs over thy head,*
> *Fine, or superfine?*

HORSES AND MEN

*

It was a hard jolt for me, one of the bitterest I ever had to face. And it all came about through my own foolishness, too. Even yet sometimes, when I think of it, I want to cry or swear or kick myself. Perhaps, even now, after all this time, there will be a kind of satisfaction in making myself look cheap by telling of it.

It began at three o'clock one October afternoon as I sat in the grand-stand at the fall trotting-and-pacing meet at Sandusky, Ohio.

To tell the truth, I felt a little foolish that I should be sitting in the grand-stand at all. During the summer before I had left my home town with Harry Whitehead and, with a nigger named Burt, had taken a job as swipe with one of the two horses Harry was campaigning through the fall race-meets that year. Mother cried and my sister Mildred, who wanted to get a job as a school-teacher in our town that fall, stormed and scolded about the house all during the week before I left. They both thought it something disgraceful that one of our family should take a place as a swipe with race-horses. I've an idea Mildred thought my taking the place would stand in the way of her getting the job she'd been working so long for.

But after all I had to work, and there was no other work to be got. A big lumbering fellow of nineteen couldn't just hang around the house and I had got too big to mow people's lawns and sell newspapers. Little chaps who could get next to people's sympathies by their sizes were always getting jobs away from me. There was one fellow who kept saying to everyone who wanted a lawn mowed or a cistern cleaned, that he was saving money to work his way through college, and I used to lay awake nights thinking up ways to injure him without being found out. I kept thinking of wagons running over him and bricks falling on his head as he walked along the street. But never mind him.

I got the place with Harry and I liked Burt fine. We got along splendid together. He was a big nigger with a lazy sprawling body and soft, kind eyes, and when it came to a fight he could hit like Jack Johnson. He had Bucephalus, a big black pacing stallion that could do 2·09 or 2·10, if he had to, and I had a little gelding named Doctor Fritz that never lost a race all fall when Harry wanted him to win.

We set out from home late in July in a box car with the two horses, and after that, until late November, we kept moving along to the race-meets and the fairs. It was a peachy time for me, I'll say that. Sometimes now I think that boys who are raised regular in houses, and never have a fine nigger like Burt for best friend, and go to high schools and college, and never steal anything, or get drunk a little, or learn to swear from fellows who know how, or come walking up in front of a grand-stand in their shirt sleeves and with dirty horsy pants on when the races are going on and the grand-stand is full of people all dressed up — What's the use of talking about it? Such fellows don't know nothing at all. They've never had no opportunity.

But I did. Burt taught me how to rub down a horse and put the bandages on after a race and steam a horse out and a lot of valuable things for any man to know. He could wrap a bandage on a horse's leg so smooth that if it had been the same colour you would think it was his skin, and I guess he'd have been a big driver, too, and got to the top like Murphy and Walter Cox and the others if he hadn't been black.

16

Gee whizz! it was fun. You got to a county seat town, maybe say on a Saturday or Sunday, and the fair began the next Tuesday and lasted until Friday afternoon. Doctor Fritz would be, say in the 2·25 trot on Tuesday afternoon, and on Thursday afternoon Bucephalus would knock 'em cold in the 'free-for-all' pace. It left you a lot of time to hang around and listen to horse talk, and see Burt knock some yap cold that got too gay, and you'd find out about horses and men and pick up a lot of stuff you could use all the rest of your life, if you had some sense and salted down what you heard and felt and saw.

And then at the end of the week when the race-meet was over, and Harry had run home to tend up to his livery-stable business, you and Burt hitched the two horses to carts and drove slow and steady across country, to the place for the next meeting, so as to not overheat the horses, etc., etc., you know.

Gee whizz! Gosh a'mighty! the nice hickory-nut and beech-nut and oaks and other kinds of trees along the roads, all brown and red, and the good smells, and Burt singing a song that was called Deep River, and the country girls at the windows of houses and everything. You can stick your colleges up your nose for all me. I guess I know where I got my education.

Why, one of those little burgs of towns you come to on the way, say now on a Saturday afternoon, and Burt says, 'Let's lay up here.' And you did.

And you took the horses to a livery stable and fed them, and you got your good clothes out of a box and put them on.

And the town was full of farmers gaping, because they could see you were race-horse people, and the kids maybe never see a nigger before and was afraid and run away when the two of us walked down their main street.

And that was before prohibition and all that foolishness, and so you went into a saloon, the two of you, and all the yaps come and stood around, and there was always someone pretended he was horsy and knew things and spoke up and began asking questions, and all you did was to lie and lie all you could about what horses you had, and I said I owned them, and then some fellow said 'Will you have a drink of whisky?' and Burt knocked his eye out the way he could say, off-hand like, 'Oh well, all right, I'm agreeable to a little nip. I'll split a quart with you.' Gee whizz!

But that isn't what I want to tell my story about. We got home late in November and I promised mother I'd quit the race-horses for good. There's a lot of things you've got to promise a mother because she don't know any better.

And so, there not being any work in our town any more than when I left there to go to the races, I went off to Sandusky and got a pretty good place taking care of horses for a man who owned a teaming and delivery and storage and coal and real-estate business there. It was a pretty good place with good eats, and a day off each week, and sleeping on a cot in a big barn, and mostly just shovelling in hay and oats to a lot of big good-enough skates of horses, that couldn't have trotted a race with a toad. I wasn't dissatisfied and I could send money home.

And then, as I started to tell you, the fall races come to Sandusky and I got the day off and I went. I left the job at noon and had on my good clothes and my new brown derby hat, I'd just bought the Saturday before, and a stand-up collar.

First of all I went down-town and walked about with the dudes. I've always thought to myself, 'Put up a good front,' and so I did it. I had forty dollars in my pocket, and so I went into the West House, a big hotel, and walked up to the cigar-stand. 'Give me three twenty-five-cent cigars,' I said. There was a lot of horsemen and strangers and dressed-up people from other towns standing around in the lobby and in the bar, and I mingled amongst them. In the bar there was a fellow with a cane and a Windsor tie on, that it made me sick to look at him. I like a man to be a man and dress up, but not to go put on that kind of airs. So I pushed him aside, kind of rough, and had me a drink of whisky. And then he looked at me, as though he thought maybe he'd get gay, but he changed his mind and didn't say anything. And then I had another drink of whisky, just to show him something, and went out and had a hack out to the races, all to myself, and when I got there I bought myself the best seat I could get up in the grand-stand, but didn't go in for any of these boxes. That's putting on too many airs.

And so there I was, sitting up in the grand-stand as gay as you please and looking down on the swipes coming out with their horses, and with their dirty horsy pants on and the horse blankets swung over their shoulders, same as I had been doing all the year before. I liked one thing about the same as the other, sitting up there and feeling grand and being down there and looking up at the yaps and feeling grander and more important, too. One thing's about as good as another, if you take it just right. I've often said that.

Well, right in front of me, in the grand-stand that day, there was a fellow with a couple of girls and they was about my age. The young fellow was a nice guy all right. He was the kind maybe that goes to college and then comes to be a lawyer or maybe a newspaper editor or something like that, but he wasn't stuck on himself. There are some of that kind are all right and he was one of the ones.

He had his sister with him and another girl and the sister looked around over his shoulder, accidental at first, not intending to start anything — she wasn't that kind — and her eyes and mine happened to meet.

You know how it is. Gee, she was a peach! She had on a soft dress, kind of a blue stuff and it looked carelessly made, but was well sewed and made and everything. I knew that much. I blushed when she looked right at me and so did she. She was the nicest girl I've ever seen in my life. She wasn't stuck on herself and she could talk proper grammar without being like a school-teacher or something like that. What I mean is, she was O.K. I think maybe her father was well-to-do, but not rich to make her chesty because she was his daughter, as some are. Maybe he owned a drugstore or a dry-goods store in their home town, or something like that. She never told me and I never asked.

My own people are all O.K., too, when you come to that. My grandfather was Welsh and over in the old country, in Wales he was — But never mind that.

The first heat of the first race come off and the young fellow sitting there with the two girls left them and went down to make a bet. I knew what he was up to, but he didn't talk big and noisy and let everyone around know he

20

was a sport, as some do. He wasn't that kind. Well, he come back and I heard him tell the two girls what horse he'd bet on, and when the heat was trotted they all half got to their feet and acted in the excited, sweaty way people do when they've got money down on a race, and the horse they bet on is up there pretty close at the end, and they think maybe he'll come on with a rush, but he never does because he hasn't got the old juice in him, come right down to it.

And then, pretty soon, the horses came out for the 2·18 pace and there was a horse in it I knew. He was a horse Bob French had in his string, but Bob didn't own him. He was a horse owned by a Mr. Mathers down at Marietta, Ohio.

This Mr. Mathers had a lot of money and owned some coal mines or something, and he had a swell place out in the country, and he was stuck on race-horses, but was a Presbyterian or something, and I think more than likely his wife was one, too, maybe a stiffer one than himself. So he never raced his horses hisself, and the story round the Ohio race-tracks was that when one of his horses got ready to go to the races he turned him over to Bob French and pretended to his wife he was sold.

So Bob had the horses and he did pretty much as he pleased and you can't blame Bob, at least, I never did. Sometimes he was out to win and sometimes he wasn't. I never cared much about that when I was swiping a horse. What I did want to know was that my horse had the speed and could go out in front, if you wanted him to.

And, as I'm telling you, there was Bob in this race with one of Mr. Mathers' horses, which was named 'About Ben Ahem' or something like that, and was fast as a streak. He was a gelding and had a mark of 2˙21, but could step in ˙08 or ˙09.

Because when Burt and I were out, as I've told you, the year before, there was a nigger, Burt knew, worked for Mr. Mathers and we went out there one day when we didn't have no race on at the Marietta Fair and our boss Harry was gone home.

And so everyone was gone to the fair but just this one nigger and he took us all through Mr. Mathers' swell house and he and Burt tapped a bottle of wine Mr. Mathers had hid in his bedroom, back in a closet, without his wife knowing, and he showed us this Ahem horse. Burt was always stuck on being a driver but didn't have much chance to get to the top, being a nigger, and he and the other nigger gulped that whole bottle of wine and Burt got a little lit up.

So the nigger let Burt take this About Ben Ahem and step him a mile in a track Mr. Mathers had all to himself, right there on the farm. And Mr. Mathers had one child, a daughter, kinda sick and not very good looking, and she came home and we had to hustle and get About Ben Ahem stuck back in the barn.

I'm only telling you to get everything straight. At Sandusky, that afternoon I was at the fair, this young fellow with the two girls was fussed, being with the girls and losing his bet. You know how a fellow is that way. One of them was his girl and the other his sister. I had figured that out.

'Gee whizz!' I says to myself, 'I'm going to give him the dope.'

He was mighty nice when I touched him on the shoulder. He and the girls were nice to me right from the start and clear to the end. I'm not blaming them.

And so he leaned back and I give him the dope on About Ben Ahem. 'Don't bet a cent on this first heat because he'll go like an oxen hitched to a plough, but when the first heat is over go right down and lay on your pile.' That's what I told him.

Well, I never saw a fellow treat anyone sweller. There was a fat man sitting beside the little girl, that had looked at me twice by this time, and I at her, and both blushing, and what did he do but have the nerve to turn and ask the fat man to get up and change places with me so I could sit with his crowd.

Gee whizz, craps a'mighty! There I was. What a chump I was to go and get gay up there in the West House bar, and just because that dude was standing there with a cane and that kind of a necktie on, to go and get all balled up and drink that whisky, just to show off.

Of course she would know, me sitting right beside her and letting her smell of my breath. I could have kicked myself right down out of that grand-stand and all around that race-track and made a faster record than most of the skates of horses they had there that year.

Because that girl wasn't any mutt of a girl. What wouldn't I have give right then for a stick of chewing-gum to chew, or a lozenger, or some liquorice, or most anything. I was glad I had those twenty-five-cent cigars in my pocket and right away I give that fellow one and lit one myself. Then that fat man got up and we changed places and there I was, plunked right down beside her.

They introduced themselves and the fellow's best girl, he had with him, was named Miss Elinor Woodbury, and her father was a manufacturer of barrels from a place called Tiffin, Ohio. And the fellow himself was named Wilbur Wessen and his sister was Miss Lucy Wessen.

I suppose it was their having such swell names got me off my trolly. A fellow, just because he has been a swipe with a race-horse, and works taking care of horses for a man in the teaming, delivery, and storage business, isn't any better or worse than anyone else. I've often thought that, and said it, too.

But you know how a fellow is. There's something in that kind of nice clothes, and the kind of nice eyes she had, and the way she had looked at me, awhile before, over her brother's shoulder, and me looking back at her, and both of us blushing.

I couldn't show her up for a boob, could I?

I made a fool of myself, that's what I did. I said my name was Walter Mathers from Marietta, Ohio, and then I told all three of them the smashingest lie you ever heard. What I said was that my father owned the horse About Ben Ahem and that he had let him out to this Bob French for racing purposes, because our family was proud and had never gone into racing that way, in our own name, I mean. Then I had got started and they were all leaning over and listening, and Miss Lucy Wessen's eyes were shining, and I went the whole hog.

I told about our place down at Marietta, and about the big stables and the grand brick house we had on a hill, up above the Ohio River, but I knew enough not to do it in no bragging way. What I did was to start things and then let them drag the rest out of me. I acted just as reluctant to tell as I could. Our family hasn't got any barrel factory, and, since I've known us, we've always been pretty poor,

but not asking anything of anyone at that, and my grandfather, over in Wales — but never mind that.

We sat there talking like we had known each other for
years and years, and I went and told them that my father
had been expecting maybe this Bob French wasn't on the
square, and had sent me up to Sandusky on the sly to find
out what I could.

And I bluffed it through I had found out all about the
2·18 pace, in which About Ben Ahem was to start.

I said he would lose the first heat by pacing like a lame
cow and then he would come back and skin 'em alive after
that. And to back up what I said I took thirty dollars out
of my pocket and handed it to Mr. Wilbur Wessen and
asked him, would he mind, after the first heat, to go down
and place it on About Ben Ahem for whatever odds he
could get. What I said was that I didn't want Bob French
to see me and none of the swipes.

Sure enough the first heat come off and About Ben
Ahem went off his stride, up the back stretch, and looked
like a wooden horse or a sick one, and come in to be last.
Then this Wilbur Wessen went down to the betting-place
under the grand-stand and there I was with the two girls,
and when that Miss Woodbury was looking the other way
once, Lucy Wessen kinda, with her shoulder you know,
kinda touched me. Not just tucking down, I don't mean.
You know how a woman can do. They get close, but
not getting gay either. You know what they do. Gee
whizz!

And then they give me a jolt. What they had done,
when I didn't know, was to get together, and they had
decided Wilbur Wessen would bet fifty dollars, and the two

girls had gone and put in ten dollars each, of their own money, too. I was sick then, but I was sicker later.

About the gelding, About Ben Ahem, and their winning their money, I wasn't worried a lot about that. It come out O.K. Ahem stepped the next three heats like a bushel of spoiled eggs going to market before they could be found out, and Wilbur Wessen had got nine to two for the money. There was something else eating at me.

Because Wilbur come back, after he had bet the money, and after that he spent most of his time talking to that Miss Woodbury, and Lucy Wessen and I was left alone together like on a desert island. Gee, if I'd only been on the square, or if there had been any way of getting myself on the square. There ain't any Walter Mathers, like I said to her and them, and there hasn't ever been one, but if there was, I bet I'd go to Marietta, Ohio, and shoot him to-morrow

There I was, big boob that I am. Pretty soon the race was over, and Wilbur had gone down and collected our money, and we had a hack down-town, and he stood us a swell supper at the West House, and a bottle of champagne beside.

And I was with that girl and she wasn't saying much, and I wasn't saying much either. One thing I know. She wasn't stuck on me because of the lie about my father being rich and all that. There's a way you know. . . . Craps a'mighty! There's a kind of girl, you see just once in your life, and if you don't get busy and make hay, then you're gone for good and all, and might as well go jump off a bridge. They give you a look from inside of them somewhere, and it ain't no vamping, and what it means is — you want that girl to be your wife, and you want nice things around her like flowers and swell clothes, and you want

26

her to have the kids you're going to have, and you want
good music played and no ragtime. Gee whizz!

There's a place over near Sandusky, across a kind of bay,
and it's called Cedar Point. And after we had supper we
went over to it in a launch, all by ourselves. Wilbur and
Miss Lucy and that Miss Woodbury had to catch a ten
o'clock train back to Tiffin, Ohio, because, when you're
out with girls like that you can't get careless and miss any
trains and stay out all night, like you can with some kinds
of Janes.

And Wilbur blowed himself to the launch, and it cost
him fifteen cold plunks, but I wouldn't never have knew if
I hadn't listened. He wasn't no tin-horn kind of a sport.

Over at the Cedar Point place, we didn't stay around
where there was a gang of common kind of cattle at all.

There was big dance-halls and dining-places for yaps,
and there was a beach you could walk along and get where
it was dark, and we went there.

She didn't talk hardly at all and neither did I, and I was
thinking how glad I was my mother was all right, and
always made us kids learn to eat with a fork at table, and
not swill soup, and not be noisy and rough like a gang you
see around a race-track that way.

Then Wilbur and his girl went away up the beach and
Lucy and I sat down in a dark place, where there was some
roots of old trees the water had washed up, and after that
the time, till we had to go back in the launch and they had
to catch their trains, wasn't nothing at all. It went like
winking your eye.

Here's how it was. The place we were sitting in was
dark, like I said, and there was the roots from that old
stump sticking up like arms, and there was a watery smell,

27

and the night was like — as if you could put your hand out and feel it — so warm and soft and dark and sweet like an orange.

I 'most cried and I 'most swore and I 'most jumped up and danced, I was so mad and happy and sad.

When Wilbur come back from being alone with his girl, and she saw him coming, Lucy she says, 'We got to go to the train now,' and she was 'most crying, too, but she never knew nothing I knew, and she couldn't be so all busted up. And then, before Wilbur and Miss Woodbury got up to where we was, she put her face up and kissed me quick and put her head up against me and she was all quivering and — Gee whizz!

Sometimes I hope I have cancer and die. I guess you know what I mean. We went in the launch across the bay to the train like that, and it was dark, too. She whispered and said it was like she and I could get out of the boat and walk on the water, and it sounded foolish, but I knew what she meant.

And then quick we were right at the depot, and there was a big gang of yaps, the kind that goes to the fairs, and crowded and milling around like cattle, and how could I tell her? 'It won't be long because you'll write and I'll write to you.' That's all she said.

I got a chance like a hay-barn afire. A swell chance I got.

And maybe she would write me, down at Marietta that way, and the letter would come back, and stamped on the front of it by the U.S.A., 'There ain't any such guy,' or something like that, whatever they stamp on a letter that way.

28

And me trying to pass myself off for a big bug and a swell – to her, as decent a little body as God ever made. Craps a'mighty – a swell chance I got!

And then the train come in, and she got on it, and Wilbur Wessen he come and shook hands with me, and that Miss Woodbury was nice, too, and bowed to me, and I at her, and the train went and I busted out and cried like a kid.

Gee, I could have run after that train and made Dan Patch look like a freight train after a wreck but, socks a'mighty, what was the use? Did you ever see such a fool?

I'll bet you what – if I had an arm broke right now or a train had run over my foot – I wouldn't go to no doctor at all. I'd go sit down and let her hurt and hurt – that's what I'd do.

I'll bet you what – if I hadn't a drunk that booze I'd a never been such a boob as to go tell such a lie – that couldn't never be made straight to a lady like her.

I wish I had that fellow right here that had on a Windsor tie and carried a cane. I'd smash him for fair. Gosh darn his eyes. He's a big fool – that's what he is.

And if I'm not another you just go find me one and I'll quit working and be a bum and give him my job. I don't care nothing for working, and earning money, and saving it for no such boob as myself.

THE TRIUMPH OF A MODERN

OR, SEND FOR THE LAWYER

*

INASMUCH as I have put to myself the task of trying to tell you a curious story in which I am myself concerned – in a strictly secondary way you must of course understand – I will begin by giving you some notion of myself.

Very well then, I am a man of thirty-two, rather small in size, with sandy hair. I wear glasses. Until two years ago I lived in Chicago, where I had a position as clerk in an office that afforded me a good enough living. I have never married, being somewhat afraid of women – in the flesh, in a way of speaking. In fancy and in my imagination I have always been very bold, but in the flesh women have always frightened me horribly. They have a way of smiling quietly as though to say – But we will not go into that now.

Since boyhood I have had an ambition to be a painter, not, I will confess, because of a desire to produce some great masterpiece of the arts, but simply and solely because I have always thought the life painters lead would appeal to me.

I have always liked the notion (let's be honest if we can) of going about, wearing a hat, tipped a little to the side of my head, sporting a moustache, carrying a cane and speaking in an off-hand way of such things as form, rhythm, the effects of light and masses, surfaces, etc., etc. During my life I have read a good many books concerning painters and their work, their friendships and their loves, and when I was in Chicago and poor and was compelled to live in a small room alone, I assure you I carried off many a dull weary evening by imagining myself a painter of wide renown in the world.

It was afternoon and having finished my day's work I went strolling off to the studio of another painter. He was still at work and there were two models in the room, women in the nude sitting about. One of them smiled at me, I thought a little wistfully, but, pshaw! I am too blasé for anything of that sort.

I go across the room to my friend's canvas and stand looking at it.

Now he is looking at me, a little anxiously. I am the greater man, you understand. That is frankly and freely acknowledged. Whatever else may be said against my friend he never claimed to be my equal. In fact, it is generally understood, wherever I go, that I am the greater man.

'Well?' says my friend. You see he is fairly hanging on my words, as the saying goes; in short, he is waiting for me to speak with the air of one about to be hanged.

Why? The devil! Why does he put everything up to me? One gets tired carrying such responsibility upon one's shoulders. A painter should be the judge of his own work and not embarrass his fellow-painters by asking questions. That is my method.

Very well then. If I speak sharply you have only yourself to blame. 'The yellow you have been using is a little muddy. The arm of this woman is not felt. In painting one should feel the arm of a woman. What I advise is that you change your palette. You have scattered too much. Pull it together. A painting should stick together as a wet snowball thrown by a boy clings to a wall.'

When I had reached the age of thirty, that is to say two years ago, I received from my aunt, the sister of my father to be exact, a small fortune I had long been dreaming I might possibly inherit.

My aunt I had never seen, but I had always been saying to myself, 'I must go to see my aunt. The old lady will be sore at me and when she dies will not leave me a cent.'

And then, lucky fellow that I am, I did go to see her just before she died.

Filled with determination to put the thing through, I set out from Chicago, and it is not my fault that I did not spend the day with her. Even although my aunt is (as I am not fool enough not to know that you know) a woman, I would have spent the day with her but that it was impossible.

She lived at Madison, Wisconsin, and I went there on Saturday morning. The house was locked and the windows boarded up. Fortunately, at just that moment, a mail carrier came along and, upon my telling him that I was my aunt's nephew, gave me her address. He also gave me some news concerning her.

For years she had been a sufferer from hay-fever and every summer had to have a change of climate.

That was an opportunity for me. I went at once to an hotel and wrote her a letter telling of my visit and expressing, to the utmost of my ability, my sorrow in not having found her at home. 'I have been a long time doing this job, but now that I am at it I fancy I shall do it rather well,' I said to myself.

A sort of feeling came into my hand, as it were. I can't just say what it was, but as soon as I sat down I knew very well I should be eloquent. For the moment I was positively a poet.

In the first place, and as one should in writing a letter

to a lady, I spoke of the sky. 'The sky is full of mottled clouds,' I said. Then, and I frankly admit in a brutally casual way, I spoke of myself as one practically prostrated with grief. To tell the truth I did not just know what I was doing. I had got the fever for writing words, you see. They fairly flowed out of my pen.

I had come, I said, on a long and weary journey to the home of my only female relative, and here I threw into the letter some reference to the fact that I was an orphan. 'Imagine,' I wrote, 'the sorrow and desolation in my heart at finding the house unoccupied and the windows boarded up.'

It was there, sitting in the hotel at Madison, Wisconsin, with the pen in my hand, that I made my fortune. Something bold and heroic came into my mood and, without a moment's hesitation, I mentioned in my letter what should never be mentioned to a woman, unless she be an elderly woman of one's own family, and then only by a physician perhaps – I spoke of my aunt's breasts, using the plural.

I had hoped, I said, to lay my tired head on her breasts. To tell the truth I had become drunken with words and now, how glad I am that I did. Mr. George Moore, Clive Bell, Paul Rosenfeld, and others of the most skilful writers of our English speech, have written a great deal about painters and, as I have already explained, there was not a book or magazine article in English and concerning painters, their lives and works, procurable in Chicago, I had not read.

What I am now striving to convey to you is something of my own pride in my literary effort in the hotel at Madison, Wisconsin, and surely, if I was, at that moment an artist, no other artist has ever had such quick and whole-hearted recognition.

Having spoken of putting my tired head on my aunt's breasts (poor woman, she died, never having seen me), I went on to give the general impression – which by the way was quite honest and correct – of a somewhat boyish figure, rather puzzled, wandering in a confused way through life. The imaginary but correct enough figure of myself, born at the moment in my imagination, had made its way through dismal swamps of gloom, over the rough hills of adversity and through the dry deserts of loneliness, toward the one spot in all this world where it had hoped to find rest and peace – that is to say upon the bosom of its aunt. However, as I have already explained, being a thorough modern and full of the modern boldness, I did not use the word bosom, as an old-fashioned writer might have done. I used the word breasts. When I had finished writing, tears were in my eyes.

The letter I wrote on that day covered some seven sheets of hotel paper – finely written to the margins – and cost four cents to mail.

'Shall I mail it or shall I not?' I said to myself as I came out of the hotel office and stood before a mail-box. The letter was balanced between my finger and thumb.

'Eeny, meeny, miny, mo,
Catch a nigger by the toe.'

The forefinger of my left hand – I was holding the letter in my right hand – touched my nose, mouth, forehead, eyes, chin, neck, shoulder, arm, hand and then tapped the letter itself. No doubt I fully intended, from the first, to drop it. I had been doing the work of an artist. Well, artists are always talking of destroying their own work but few do it, and those who do are perhaps the real heroes of life.

And so down into the mail-box it went with a thud and my fortune was made. The letter was received by my aunt, who was lying abed of an illness that was to destroy her – she had, it seems, other things beside hay-fever the matter with her – and she altered her will in my favour. She had intended leaving her money, a tidy sum yielding an income of five thousand a year, to a fund to be established for the study of methods for the cure of hay-fever – that is to say, really you see, to her fellow-sufferers – but instead left it to me. My aunt could not find her spectacles, and a nurse – may the gods bring her bright days and a good husband – read the letter aloud. Both women were deeply touched and my aunt wept. I am only telling you the facts, you understand, but I would like to suggest that this whole incident might well be taken as proof of the power of modern art. From the first I have been a firm believer in the moderns. I am one who, as an art critic might word it, has been right down through the movements. At first I was an impressionist and later a cubist, a post-impressionist, and even a vorticist. Time after time, in my imaginary life, as a painter, I have been quite swept off my feet. For example, I remember Picasso's blue period . . . but we'll not go into that.

What I am trying to say is that, having this faith in modernity, if one may use the word thus, I did find within myself a peculiar boldness as I sat in the hotel writing-room at Madison, Wisconsin. I used the word breasts (in the plural, you understand), and everyone will admit that it is a bold and modern word to use in a letter to an aunt one has never seen. It brought my aunt and me into one family. Her modesty never could have admitted anything else.

And then, my aunt was really touched. Afterward I talked to the nurse and made her a rather handsome present for her part in the affair. When the letter had been read my aunt felt overwhelmingly drawn to me. She turned her face to the wall and her shoulders shook. Do not think that I am not also touched as I write this. 'Poor lad,' my aunt said to the nurse, 'I will make things easier for him. Send for the lawyer.'

*

THERE was one time in Tom's life when he came near dying, came so close to it that for several days he held his own life in his hand, as a boy would hold a ball. He had only to open his fingers to let it drop.

How vividly I remember the night when he told me the story. We had gone to dine together at a little combined saloon and restaurant in what is now Wells Street in Chicago. It was a wet cold night in early October. In Chicago, October and November are usually the most charming months of the year, but that year the first weeks of October were cold and rainy. Everyone who lives in our industrial lake cities has a disease of the nasal passages and a week of such weather starts everyone coughing and sneezing. The warm little den into which Tom and I had got seemed cosy and comfortable. We had drinks of whisky to drive the chill out of our bodies and then, after eating, Tom began to talk.

Something had come into the air of the place where we sat, a kind of weariness. At times all Chicagoans grow weary of the almost universal ugliness of Chicago and everyone sags. One feels it in the streets, in the stores, in the homes. The bodies of the people sag, and a cry seems to go up out of a million throats – 'We are set down here in this continual noise, dirt and ugliness. Why did you put us down here? There is no rest. We are always being hurried about from place to place, to no end. Millions of us live on the vast Chicago West Side, where all streets are equally ugly and where the streets go on and on for ever, out of nowhere into nothing. We are tired, tired! What is it all about? Why did you put us down here, mother of men?' All the moving bodies of the people in the streets seem to be saying something like the words set down above and some day, perhaps, that Chicago poet, Carl Sandburg, will sing a song about it. Oh, he will make you feel then the tired voices coming out of tired people. Then, it may be, we will all begin singing it and realizing something long forgotten among us.

But I grow too eloquent. I will return to Tom and the restaurant in Wells Street. Carl Sandburg works on a newspaper and sits at a desk writing about the movies in Wells Street, Chicago.

In the restaurant two men stood at the bar talking to the bartender. They were trying to hold a friendly conversation, but there was something in the air that made friendly conversations impossible. The bartender looked like pictures one sees of famous generals – he was the type – a red-faced-, well-fed-looking man, with a grey moustache.

The two men facing him and with their feet resting on the bar rail had got into a meaningless wrangle concerning the relationship of President McKinley and his friend Mark Hanna. Did Mark Hanna control McKinley or was McKinley only using Mark Hanna to his own ends? The discussion was of no special interest to the men engaged in it – they did not care. At that time the newspapers and political magazines of the country were always wrangling over the same subject. It filled space that had to be filled, I should say.

At any rate, the two men had taken it up and were using it as a vehicle for their weariness and disgust with life. They spoke of McKinley and Hanna as Bill and Mark.

'Bill is a smooth one, I tell you what. He has Mark eating out of his hand '

38

'Eating out of his hand, hell! Mark whistles and Bill comes running, like that, like a little dog.'

Meaningless, vicious sentences, opinions thrown out by tired brains. One of the men grew sullenly angry. 'Don't look at me like that, I tell you. I'll stand a good deal from a friend but not any such looks. I'm a fellow who loses his temper. Sometimes I bust someone on the jaw.'

The bartender was taking the situation in hand. He tried to change the subject. 'Who's going to lick that Fitz-simmons? How long they going to let that Australian strut around in this country? Ain't they no guy can take him?' he asked, with pumped-up enthusiasm.

I sat with my head in my hands. 'Men jangling with men! Men and women in houses and apartments jangling! Tired people going home to Chicago's West Side, going home from the factories! Children crying fretfully!'

Tom tapped me on the shoulder, and then tapped with his empty glass on the table. He laughed.

'Ladybug, ladybug, why do you roam?
Ladybug, ladybug, fly away home,'

he recited. When the whisky had come he leaned forward and made one of the odd and truthful observations on life that were always coming out of him at unexpected moments. 'I want you to notice something,' he began. 'You have seen a lot of bartenders – well, if you'll notice, there is a striking similarity in appearance between bar-tenders, great generals, diplomats, presidents and all such people. I just happened to think why it is. It's because they are all up to the same game. They have to spend their lives handling weary dissatisfied people and they learn the trick of giving things just a little twist, out of one dull meaningless channel into another. That is their game and practising it makes them all look alike.'

I smiled sympathetically. Now that I come to write of my friend I find it somewhat difficult not to misrepresent him on the sentimental side. I forget times when I was with him and he was unspeakably dull, when he also talked often for hours of meaningless things. It was all foolishness, this trying to be anything but a dull business man, he sometimes said, and declared that both he and I were fools. Better for us both that we become more alert, more foxy, as he put it. But for the fact that we were both fools we would both join the Chicago Athletic Club, play golf, ride about in automobiles, pick up flashy young girls and take them out to road-houses to dinner, go home later and make up cock-and-bull stories to quiet our wives, go home to church on Sunday, talk continuously of money-making, woman and golf, and in general enjoy our lives. At times he half convinced me he thought the fellows he described led gay and cheerful lives.

And there were times, too, when he, as a physical being, seemed to fairly disintegrate before my eyes. His great bulk grew a little loose and flabby, he talked and talked, saying nothing.

And then, when I had quite made up my mind he had gone the same road I and all the men about me were no doubt going, the road of surrender to ugliness and to dreary, meaningless living, something would happen. He would have talked thus, as I have just described, aimlessly, through a long evening, and then, when we parted for the night, he would scribble a few words on a bit of paper and push it awkwardly into my pocket. I watched his

40

lumbering figure go away along a street and going to a
street lamp read what he had written.

'I am very weary. I am not the silly ass I seem, but I
am as tired as a dog, trying to find out what I am,' were
the words he had scrawled.

But to return to the evening in the place in Wells
Street. When the whisky came we drank it and sat looking at each other. Then he put his hand on the table and
closing the fingers, so that they made a little cup, opened
the hand slowly and listlessly. 'Once I had life, like that,
in my hand, my own life. I could have let go of it as easily
as that. Just why I didn't I've never quite figured out.
I can't think why I kept my fingers cupped, instead of
opening my hand and letting go,' he said. If, a few
minutes before, there had been no integrity in the man
there was enough of it now.

He began telling the story of an evening and a night of
his youth.

It was when he was still on his father's farm, a little
rented farm down in South-eastern Ohio, and when he was
but eighteen years old. That would have been in the fall
before he left home and started on his adventures in the
world. I knew something of his history.

It was late October and he and his father had been
digging potatoes in a field. I suppose they both wore torn
shoes as, in telling the story, Tom made a point of the fact
that their feet were cold, and that the black dirt had
worked into their shoes and discoloured their feet.

The day was cold and Tom wasn't very well and was
in a bitter mood. He and his father worked rather desperately and in silence. The father was tall, had a sallow
complexion and wore a beard, and in the mental picture I

have of him, he is always stopping – as he walks about the farmyard or works in the field he stops and runs his fingers nervously through his beard.

As for Tom, one gets the notion of him as having been at that time rather nice, one having an inclination toward the nicer things of life without just knowing he had the feeling, and certainly without an opportunity to gratify it.

Tom had something the matter with him, a cold with a bit of fever perhaps, and sometimes as he worked his body shook as with a chill and then, after a few minutes, he felt hot all over. The two men had been digging the potatoes all afternoon and as night began to fall over the field, they started to pick up. One picks up the potatoes in baskets and carries them to the ends of the rows where they are put into two-bushel grain-bags.

Tom's stepmother came to the kitchen door and called. 'Supper,' she cried in her peculiarly colourless voice. Her husband was a little angry and fretful. Perhaps for a long time he had been feeling very deeply the enmity of his son. 'All right,' he called back, 'we'll come pretty soon. We got to get done picking up.' There was something very like a whine in his voice. 'You can keep the things hot for a time,' he shouted.

Tom and his father both worked with feverish haste, as though trying to outdo each other, and every time Tom bent over to pick up a handful of the potatoes his head whirled and he thought he might fall. A kind of terrible pride had taken possession of him and with the whole strength of his being he was determined not to let his father – who, if ineffectual, was nevertheless sometimes very quick and accurate at tasks – get the better of him. They were picking up potatoes – that was the task before them at the moment – and the thing was to get all the potatoes picked up and in the bags before darkness came. Tom did not believe in his father, and was he to let such an ineffectual man outdo him at any task, no matter how ill he might be?

That was somewhat the nature of Tom's thoughts and feelings at the moment.

And then the darkness had come and the task was done. The filled sacks were set along a fence at the end of the field. It was to be a cold frosty night and now the moon was coming up and the filled sacks looked like grotesque human beings, standing there along the fence – standing with grey sagging bodies, such as Tom's stepmother had – sagged bodies and dull eyes – standing and looking at the two men, so amazingly not in accord with each other.

As the two walked across the field Tom let his father go ahead. He was afraid he might stagger and did not want his father to see there was anything the matter with him. In a way boyish pride was involved, too. 'He might think he could wear me out working,' Tom thought. The moon coming up was a huge yellow ball in the distance. It was larger than the house toward which they were walking and the figure of Tom's father seemed to walk directly across the yellow face of the moon.

When they got to the house the children Tom's father had got – thrown in with the woman, as it were, when he made his second marriage – were standing about. After he left home Tom could never remember anything about the children except that they always had dirty faces and were clad in torn dirty dresses and that the youngest, a baby, wasn't very well and was always crying fretfully.

When the two men came into the house the children,

from having been fussing at their mother because the meal was delayed, grew silent. With the quick intuition of children they sensed something wrong between father and son. Tom walked directly across the small dining-room and opening a door entered a stairway that led up to his bedroom.

'Ain't you going to eat any supper?' his father asked. It was the first word that had passed between father and son for hours.

'No,' Tom answered and went up the stairs. At the moment his mind was concentrated on the problem of not letting anyone in the house know he was ill, and the father let him go without protest. No doubt the whole family were glad enough to have him out of the way.

He went upstairs and into his own room and got into bed without taking off his clothes, just pulled off the torn shoes and crawling in pulled the covers up over himself. There was an old quilt, not very clean.

His brain cleared a little and as the house was small he could hear everything going on downstairs. Now the family were all seated at the table and his father was doing a thing called 'saying grace.' He always did that, and sometimes, while the others waited, he prayed intermittently.

Tom was thinking, trying to think. What was it all about, his father's praying that way? When he got at it the man seemed to forget everyone else in the world. There he was, alone with God, facing God alone and the people about him seemed to have no existence. He prayed a little about food, and then went on to speak with God, in a strange confidential way, about other things, his own frustrated desires mostly.

All his life he had wanted to be a Methodist minister

but could not be ordained because he was uneducated, had never been to the schools or colleges. There was no chance at all for his becoming just the thing he wanted to be and still he went on and on praying about it, and in a way seemed to think there might be a possibility that God, feeling strongly the need of more Methodist ministers, would suddenly come down out of the sky, off the judgment seat as it were, and would go to the administrating board, or whatever one might call it, of the Methodist Church and say, 'Here you, what are you up to? Make this man a Methodist minister and be quick about it. I don't want any fooling around.'

Tom lay on the bed upstairs listening to his father praying down below. When he was a lad and his own mother was alive he had always been compelled to go with his father to the church on Sundays and to the prayer-meetings on Wednesday evenings. His father always prayed, delivered sermons to the other sad-faced men and women sitting about, under the guise of prayers, and the son sat listening and no doubt it was then, in childhood, his hatred of his father was born. The man who was then the minister of the little country church, a tall, raw-boned young man, who was as yet unmarried, sometimes spoke of Tom's father as one powerful in prayer.

And all the time there was something in Tom's mind. Well, he had seen a thing. One day when he was walking alone through a strip of wood, coming back barefooted from town to the farm he had seen – he never told anyone what he had seen. The minister was in the wood, sitting alone on a log. There was something. Some rather nice sense of life in Tom was deeply offended. He had crept away unseen.

45

And now he was lying on the bed in the half darkness upstairs in his father's house, shaken with a chill, and downstairs his father was praying and there was one sentence always creeping into his prayers. 'Give me the gift, O God, give me the great gift.' Tom thought he knew what that meant – 'The gift of the gab and the opportunity to exercise it, eh?'

There was a door at the foot of Tom's bed and beyond the door another room, at the front of the house upstairs. His father slept in there with the new woman he had married and the three children slept in a small room beside it. The baby slept with the man and woman. It was odd what terrible thoughts sometimes came into one's head. The baby wasn't very well and was always whining and crying. Chances were it would grow up to be a yellow-skinned thing, with dull eyes, like the mother. Suppose . . . well, suppose . . . some night . . . one did not voluntarily have such thoughts – suppose either the man or woman might, quite accidentally, roll over on the baby and crush it, smother it, rather.

Tom's mind slipped a little out of his grasp. He was trying to hold on to something – what was it? Was it his own life? That was an odd thought. Now his father had stopped praying and downstairs the family were eating the evening meal. There was silence in the house. People, even dirty, half-ill children, grew silent when they ate. That was a good thing. It was good to be silent some-times.

And now Tom was in the wood, going barefooted through the wood, and there was that man, the minister, sitting alone there on the log. Tom's father wanted to be a minister, wanted God to arbitrarily make him a minister, wanted God to break the rules, bust up the regular order of things just to make him a minister. And he a man who could barely make a living on the farm, who did everything in a half-slipshod way, who, when he felt he had to have a second wife, had gone off and got one with four sickly kids, one who couldn't cook, who did the work of his house in a slovenly way.

Tom slipped off into unconsciousness and lay still for a long time. Perhaps he slept.

When he awoke – or came back into consciousness – there was his father's voice still praying and Tom had thought the grace-saying was over. He lay still, listening. The voice was loud and insistent and now seemed near at hand. All of the rest of the house was silent. None of the children were crying.

Now there was a sound, the rattling of dishes downstairs in the kitchen and Tom sat up in bed and leaning far over looked through the open door into the room occupied by his father and his father's new wife. His mind cleared.

After all, the evening meal was over and the children had been put to bed and now the woman downstairs had put the three older children into their bed and was washing the dishes at the kitchen stove. Tom's father had come upstairs and had prepared for bed by taking off his clothes and putting on a long soiled white nightgown. Then he had gone to the open window at the front of the house and kneeling down had begun praying again.

A kind of cold fury took possession of Tom and without a moment's hesitation he got silently out of bed. He did not feel ill now but very strong. At the foot of his bed, leaning against the wall, was a whippletree, a round piece

47

of hard wood, shaped something like a baseball bat, but tapering at both ends. At each end there was an iron ring. The whippletree had been left there by his father, who was always leaving things about, in odd unexpected places. He leaned a whippletree against the wall in his son's bedroom and then, on the next day, when he was hitching a horse to a plough and wanted it, he spent hours going nervously about rubbing his fingers through his beard and looking.

Tom took the whippletree in his hand and crept barefooted through the open door into his father's room. 'He wants to be like that fellow in the woods – that's what he's always praying about.' There was in Tom's mind some notion – from the beginning there must have been a great deal of the autocrat in him – well, you see, he wanted to crush out impotence and sloth.

He had quite made up his mind to kill his father with the whippletree and crept silently across the floor, gripping the hardwood stick firmly in his right hand. The sickly looking baby had already been put into the one bed in the room and was asleep. Its little face looked out from above another dirty quilt and the clear cold moonlight streamed into the room and fell upon the bed and upon the kneeling figure on the floor by the window.

Tom had got almost across the room when he noticed something – his father's bare feet sticking out from beneath the white nightgown. The heels and the little balls of flesh below the toes were black with the dirt of the fields, but in the centre of each foot there was a place. It was not black but yellowish-white in the moonlight.

Tom crept silently back into his own room and closed softly the door between himself and his father. After all

48

he did not want to kill anyone. His father had not thought it necessary to wash his feet before kneeling to pray to his God, and he had himself come upstairs and had got into bed without washing his own feet.

His hands were trembling now and his body shaking with the chill, but he sat on the edge of the bed trying to think. When he was a child and went to church with his father and mother there was a story he had heard told. A man came into a feast, after walking a long time on dusty roads, and sat down at the feast. A woman came and washed his feet. Then she put precious ointments on them and later dried the feet with her hair.

The story had, when he heard it, no special meaning to the boy, but now . . . He sat on the bed smiling half foolishly. Could one make of one's own hands a symbol of what the woman's hands must have meant on that occasion, long ago? could not one make one's own hands the humble servants to one's soiled feet, to one's soiled body?

It was a strange notion, this business of making oneself the keeper of the clean integrity of oneself. When one was ill one got things a little distorted. In Tom's room there was a tin wash-basin, and a pail of water he himself brought each morning from the cistern at the back of the house. He had always been one who fancied waiting on himself and perhaps, at that time, he had in him something he afterward lost, or only got hold of again at long intervals, the sense of the worth of his own young body, the feeling that his own body was a temple, as one might put it.

At any rate, he must have had some such feeling on that night of his childhood and I shall never forget a kind of illusion I had concerning him that time in the Wells Street place when he told me the tale. At the moment something seemed to spring out of his great hulking body, something young, hard, clean and white.

But I must walk carefully. Perhaps I had better stick to my tale, try only to tell it simply, as he did.

Anyway, he got off the bed, there in the upper room of that strangely disorganized and impotent household, and standing in the centre of the room took off his clothes. There was a towel hanging on a hook on the wall but it wasn't very clean.

By chance he did have, however, a white nightgown that had not been worn and he now got it out of the drawer of a small rickety dresser that stood by the wall and recklessly tore off a part of it to serve as a washcloth. Then he stood up and with the tin wash-basin on the floor at his feet washed himself carefully in the icy-cold water.

No matter what illusions I may have had regarding him when he told me the tale, that night in Wells Street, surely on that night of his youth he must have been, as I have already described him, something young, hard, clean and white. Surely, and at that moment, his body was a temple.

As for the matter of his holding his own life in his hands — that came later, when he had got back into the bed, and the part of his tale I do not exactly understand. Perhaps he fumbled it in the telling and perhaps my own understanding fumbled.

I remember that he kept his hand lying on the table in the Wells Street place and that he kept opening and closing the fingers as though that would explain everything. It didn't for me, not then, at any rate. Perhaps it will for you who read.

'I got back into bed,' he said, 'and taking my own life into my hand tried to decide whether I wanted to hold on to it or not. All that night I held it like that, my own life, I mean,' he said.

There was some notion, he was evidently trying to explain, concerning other lives being things outside his own, things not to be touched, not to be fooled with. How much of that could have been in his mind that night of his youth, long ago, and how much came later I do not know and one takes it for granted he did not know either.

He seemed however to have had the notion that for some hours that night, after his father's wife came upstairs and the two elder people got into bed and the house was silent, that there came certain hours when his own life belonged to him to hold or to drop as easily as one spreads out the fingers of a hand lying on a table in a saloon in Wells Street, Chicago.

'I had a fancy not to do it,' he said, 'not to spread out my fingers, not to open my hand. You see, I couldn't feel any very definite purpose in life, but there was something. There was a feeling I had as I stood naked in the cold washing my body. Perhaps I just wanted to have that feeling of washing myself again some time. You know what I mean – I was really cleansing myself, there in the moonlight, that night.

'And so I got back into bed and kept my fingers closed, like this, like a cup. I held my own life in my hand and when I felt like opening my fingers and letting my life slip away I remembered myself washing myself in the moonlight.

'And so I didn't open out my fingers. I kept my fingers

closed like this, like a cup,' he said, again slowly drawing his fingers together.

PART TWO

For a good many years Tom wrote advertisements in an office in Chicago where I was also employed. He had grown middle-aged and was unmarried and in the evenings and on Sundays sat in his apartment reading or playing rather badly on a piano. Outside business hours he had few associates, and although his youth and young manhood had been a time of hardship, he continually, in fancy, lived in the past.

He and I had been intimate, in a loose, detached sort of way, for a good many years. Although I was a much younger man we often got half-drunk together.

Little fluttering tag-like ends of his personal history were always leaking out of him and, of all the men and women I have known, he gave me the most material for stories. His own talks, things remembered or imagined, were never quite completely told. They were fragments caught up, tossed in the air as by a wind and then abruptly dropped.

All during the late afternoon we had been standing together at a bar and drinking. We had talked of our work, and as Tom grew more drunken he played with the notion of the importance of advertising-writing. At that time his more mature point of view puzzled me a little. 'I'll tell you what, that lot of advertisements on which you are now at work is very important. Do put all your best self into your work. It is very important that the American house-wife should buy Star laundry soap, rather than Arrow laundry soap. And there is something else – the daughter

52

of the man who owns the soap factory, that is at present indirectly employing you, is a very pretty girl. I saw her once. She is nineteen now but soon she will be out of college and, if her father makes a great deal of money, it will profoundly affect her life. The very man she is to marry may be decided by the success or failure of the advertisements you are now writing. In an obscure way you are fighting her battles. Like a knight of old you have tipped your lance, or shall I say typewriter, in her service. To-day as I walked past your desk and saw you sitting there, scratching your head, and trying to think whether to say, "Buy Star Laundry Soap – it's best," or whether to be a bit slangy and say, "Buy Star – You win!" – well, I say, my heart went out to you and to this fair young girl you have never seen, may never see. I tell you what, I was touched.' He hiccoughed, and leaning forward tapped me affectionately on the shoulder. 'I tell you what, young fellow,' he added, smiling, 'I thought of the Middle Ages and of the men, women and children who once set out toward the Holy Land in the service of the Virgin. They didn't get as well paid as you do. I tell you what, we advertising men are too well paid. There would be more dignity in our profession if we went barefooted and walked about dressed in old ragged cloaks and carrying staffs. We might, with a good deal more dignity, carry beggar's bowls, in our hands, eh!'

He was laughing heartily now, but suddenly stopped laughing. There was always an element of sadness in Tom's mirth.

We walked out of the saloon, he going forward a little unsteadily for, even when he was quite sober, he was not too steady on his legs. Life did not express itself very definitely in his body and he rolled awkwardly about, his heavy body at times threatening to knock some passer-by off the sidewalk.

For a time we stood at a corner, at La Salle and Lake Streets in Chicago, and about us surged the home-going crowds while over our heads rattled the elevated trains. Bits of newspaper and clouds of dust were picked up by a wind and blown in our faces and the dust got into our eyes. We laughed together, a little nervously.

At any rate, for us the evening had just begun. We would walk and later dine together. He plunged again into the saloon out of which we had just come, and in a moment returned with a bottle of whisky in his pocket.

'It is horrible stuff, this whisky, eh? but after all this is a horrible town. One couldn't drink wine here. Wine belongs to a sunny, laughing people and clime,' he said. He had a notion that drunkenness was necessary to men in such a modern industrial city as the one in which we lived. 'You wait,' he said, 'you'll see what will happen. One of these days the reformers will manage to take whisky away from us, and what then? We'll sag down, you see. We'll become like old women, who have had too many children. We'll all sag spiritually and then you'll see what'll happen. Without whisky no people can stand up against all this ugliness. It can't be done, I say. We'll become empty and bag-like – we will – all of us. We'll be like old women who were never loved but who have had too many children.'

We had walked through many streets and had come to a bridge over a river. It was growing dark now and we stood for a time in the dusk and in the uncertain light the structures, built to the very edge of the stream, great warehouses and factories, began to take on strange shapes. The river ran through a cañon formed by the buildings, a few boats passed up and down, and over other bridges, in the distance, street-cars passed. They were like moving clusters of stars against the dark purple of the sky.

From time to time he sucked at the whisky bottle and occasionally offered me a drink, but often he forgot me and drank alone. When he had taken the bottle from his lips he held it before him and spoke to it softly, 'Little mother,' he said, 'I am always at your breast, eh? You cannot wean me, can you?'

He grew a little angry. 'Well, then why did you drop me down here? Mothers should drop their children in places where men have learned a little to live. Here there is only a desert of buildings.'

He took another drink from the bottle and then held it for a moment against his cheek before passing it to me. 'There is something feminine about a whisky bottle,' he declared. 'As long as it contains liquor one hates to part with it, and passing it to a friend is a little like inviting a friend to go in to your wife. They do that, I'm told, in some of the Oriental countries – a rather delicate custom. Perhaps they are more civilized than ourselves, and then, you know, perhaps, it's just possible, they have found out that the women sometimes like it, too, eh?'

I tried to laugh but did not succeed very well. Now that I am writing of my friend, I find I am not making a very good likeness of him after all. It may be that I overdo the note of sadness I get into my account of him. There was always that element present, but it was tempered in him, as I seem to be unable to temper it in my account of him.

For one thing he was not very clever and I seem to be

making him out a rather clever fellow. On many evenings I have spent with him he was silent and positively dull and for hours walked awkwardly along, talking of some affair at the office. There was a long rambling story. He had been at Detroit with the president of the company and the two men had visited an advertiser. There was a long dull account of what had been said – of 'he saids,' and 'I saids.'

Or again he told a story of some experience of his own, as a newspaper man, before he got into advertising. He had been on the copy desk in some Chicago newspaper, the *Tribune*, perhaps. One grew accustomed to a little peculiarity of his mind. It travelled sometimes in circles and there were certain oft-told tales always bobbing up. A man had come into the newspaper office, a cub reporter with an important piece of news, a great scoop in fact. No one would believe the reporter's story. He was just a kid. There was a murderer, for whom the whole town was on the watch-out, and the cub reporter had picked him up and had brought him into the office.

There he sat, the dangerous murderer. The cub reporter had found him in a saloon and going up to him had said, 'You might as well give yourself up. They will get you, anyway, and it will go better with you if you come in voluntarily.'

And so the dangerous murderer had decided to come, and the cub reporter had escorted him, not to the police station but to the newspaper office. It was a great scoop. In a moment now the forms would close, the newspaper would go to press. The dead line was growing close and the cub reporter ran about the room from one man to another. He kept pointing at the murderer, a mild-looking little man with blue eyes, sitting on a bench, waiting. The cub reporter was almost insane. He danced up and down and shouting, 'I tell you that's Murdock, sitting there. Don't be a lot of damn fools. I tell you that's Murdock, sitting there.'

Now one of the editors has walked listlessly across the room and is speaking to the little man with blue eyes, and suddenly the whole tone of the newspaper office has changed. 'My God! It's the truth! Stop everything! Clear the front page! My God! It is Murdock! What a near thing! We almost let it go! My God! It's Murdock!'

The incident in the newspaper office had stayed in my friend's mind. It swam about in his mind as in a pool. At recurring times, perhaps once every six months, he told the story, using always the same words and the tenseness of that moment in the newspaper office was reproduced in him over and over. He grew excited. Now the men in the office were all gathering about the little blue-eyed Murdock. He had killed his wife, her lover and three children. Then he had run into the street and quite wantonly shot two men, innocently passing the house. He sat talking quietly and all the police of the city, and all the reporters for the other newspapers, were looking for him. There he sat talking, nervously telling his story. There wasn't much to the story. 'I did it. I just did it. I guess I was off my nut,' he kept saying.

'Well, the story will have to be stretched out.' The cub reporter who has brought him in walks about the office proudly. 'I've done it! I've done it! I've proven myself the greatest newspaper man in the city.' The older men are laughing. 'The fool! It's fool's luck. If he hadn't been a fool he would never have done it. Why he walked right up. "Are you Murdock?" He had gone about all over town, into saloons, asking men, "Are you Murdock?" God is good to fools and drunkards!'

My friend told the story to me ten, twelve, fifteen times, and did not know it had grown to be an old story. When he had reproduced the scene in the newspaper office he made always the same comment. 'It's a good yarn, eh? Well, it's the truth. I was there. Someone ought to write it up for one of the magazines.'

I looked at him, watched him closely as he told the story, and as I grew older and kept hearing the murderer's story and certain others, he also told regularly without knowing he had told them before, an idea came to me. 'He is a tale-teller who has had no audience,' I thought. 'He is a stream dammed up. He is full of stories that whirl and circle about within him. Well, he is not a stream dammed up, he is a stream overfull.' As I walked beside him and heard again the story of the cub reporter and the murderer I remembered a creek back of my father's house in an Ohio town. In the spring the water overflowed a field near our house and the brown muddy water ran round and round in crazy circles. One threw a stick into the water and it was carried far away but, after a time, it came whirling back to where one stood on a piece of high ground, watching.

What interested me was that the untold stories, or rather the uncompleted stories of my friend's mind, did not seem to run in circles. When a story had attained form it had to be told about every so often, but the unformed fragments were satisfied to peep out at one and then retire, never to reappear.

It was a spring evening and he and I had gone for a

walk in Jackson Park. We went on a street-car and when we were alighting the car started suddenly and my awkward friend was thrown to the ground and rolled over and over in the dusty street. The motor-man, the conductor and several of the men passengers alighted and gathered about. No, he was not hurt and would not give his name and address to the anxious conductor. 'I'm not hurt. I'm not going to sue the company. Damn it, man, I defy you to make me give my name and address if I do not care to do so.'

He assumed a look of outraged dignity. 'Just suppose now that I happen to be some great man, travelling about the country – in foreign parts, incognito, as it were. Let us suppose I am a great prince or a dignitary of some sort. Look how big I am.' He pointed to his huge round paunch. 'If I told who I was, cheers might break forth. I do not care for that. With me, you see, it is different than with yourselves. I have had too much of that sort of thing already. I'm sick of it. If it happens that, in the process of my study of the customs of your charming country, I chose to fall off a street-car that is my own affair. I did not fall on anyone.'

We walked away leaving the conductor, the motor-man and passengers somewhat mystified. 'Ah, he's a nut,' I heard one of the passengers say to another.

As for the fall, it had shaken something out of my friend. When later we were seated on a bench in the park one of the fragments, the little illuminating bits of his personal history, that sometimes came from him and that were his chief charm for me, seemed to have been shaken loose and fell from him as a ripe apple falls from a tree in a wind.

He began talking, a little hesitatingly, as though feeling his way in the darkness along the hallway of a strange house at night. It had happened I had never seen him with a woman and he seldom spoke of women, except with a witty and half-scornful gesture, but now he began speaking of an experience with a woman.

The tale concerned an adventure of his young manhood and occurred after his mother had died and after his father married again – in fact, after he had left home, not to return.

The enmity that seemed always to have existed between himself and his father became, while he continued living at home, more and more pronounced, but on the part of the son, my friend, it was never expressed in words, and his dislike of his father took the form of contempt that he had made so bad a second marriage. The new woman in the house seemed such a poor stick. The house was always dirty and the children, some other man's children, were always about under foot. When the two men who had been working in the fields came into the house to eat, the food was badly cooked.

The father's desire to have God make him, in some mysterious way, a Methodist minister continued and, as he grew older, the son had difficulty keeping back certain sharp comments upon life in the house that wanted to be expressed. 'What was a Methodist minister after all?' The son was filled with the intolerance of youth. His father was a labourer, a man who had never been to school. Did he think that God could suddenly make him something else and that without effort on his own part, by this interminable praying? If he had really wanted to be a minister why had he not prepared himself? He had chased off and

got married and when his first wife died he could hardly
wait until she was buried before making another marriage.
And what a poor stick of a woman he had got.

The son looked across the table at his stepmother who
was afraid of him. Their eyes met and the woman's hands
began to tremble.

'Do you want anything?' she asked anxiously.

'No,' he replied and began eating in silence.

One day in the spring, when he was working in the
field with his father, he decided to start out into the world.
He and his father were planting corn. They had no corn-
planter, and the father had marked out the rows with a
home-made marker and now he was going along in his
bare feet, dropping the grains of corn, and the son, with a
hoe in his hand, was following. The son drew earth over
the corn and then patted the spot with the back of the hoe.
That was to make the ground solid above so that the crows
would not come down and find the corn before it had time
to take root.

All morning the two worked in silence, and then at
noon, and when they came to the end of a row, they stopped
to rest. The father went into a fence-corner.

The son was nervous. He sat down and then got up
and walked about. He did not want to look into the fence-
corner, where his father was no doubt kneeling and praying – he was always doing that at odd moments – but
presently he did. Dread crept over him. His father was
kneeling and praying in silence and the son could see again
the bottoms of his two bare feet, sticking out from among
low-growing bushes. Tom shuddered. Again he saw the
heels and the cushions of the feet, the two ball-like cushions
below the toes. They were black, but the instep of each

foot was white with an odd whiteness – not unlike the whiteness of the belly of a fish.

The reader will understand what was in Tom's mind – a memory.

Without a word to his father or to his father's wife, he walked across the fields to the house, packed a few belongings and left, saying good-bye to no one. The woman of the house saw him go but said nothing, and after he had disappeared, about a bend in the road, she ran across the fields to her husband, who was still at his prayers, oblivious to what had happened. His wife also saw the bare feet sticking out of the bushes and ran toward them screaming. When her husband arose she began to cry hysterically. 'I thought something dreadful had happened, oh, I thought something dreadful had happened,' she sobbed.

'Why, what's the matter – what's the matter?' asked her husband; but she did not answer but ran and threw herself into his arms, and as the two stood thus, like two grotesque bags of grain, embracing in a black newly ploughed field under a grey sky, the son, who had stopped in a small clump of trees, saw them. He walked to the edge of a wood and stood for a moment and then went off along the road. Afterward he never saw or heard from them again.

About Tom's woman adventure – he told it as I have told you the story of his departure from home, that is to say in a fragmentary way. The story, like the one I have just tried to tell, or rather perhaps give you a sense of, was told in broken sentences, dropped between long silences. As my friend talked I sat looking at him and I will admit I sometimes found myself thinking he must be the greatest man I would ever know. 'He has felt more things, has by his capacity for silently feeling things, penetrated farther into human life than any other man I am likely ever to know, perhaps than any other man who lives in my day,' I thought – deeply stirred.

And so he was on the road now and working his way slowly along afoot through Southern Ohio. He intended to make his way to some city and begin educating himself. In the winter, during boyhood, he had attended a country school, but there were certain things he wanted he could not find in the country, books, for one thing. 'I knew then, as I know now, something of the importance of books, that is to say real books. There are only a few such books in the world and it takes a long time to find them out. Hardly anyone knows what they are and one of the reasons I have never married is because I did not want some woman coming between me and the search for the books that really have something to say,' he explained. He was for ever breaking the thread of his stories with little comments of this kind.

All during that summer he worked on the farms, staying sometimes for two or three weeks and then moving on, and in June he had got to a place, some twenty miles west of Cincinnatti, where he went to work on the farm of a German, and where the adventure happened that he told me about that night on the park bench.

The farm on which he was at work belonged to a tall, solidly built German of fifty, who had come to America twenty years before, and who, by hard work, had prospered and had acquired much land. Three years before he had made up his mind he had better marry and had written to a friend in Germany about getting him a wife. 'I do not want one of these American girls, and I would like a young woman, not an old one,' he wrote. He explained that the American girls all had the idea in their heads that they could run their husbands, and that most of them succeeded. 'It's getting so all they want is to ride around all dressed up or trot off to town,' he said. Even the older American women he employed as housekeepers were the same way; none of them would take hold, help about the farm, feed the stock and do things the wife of a European farmer expected to do. When he employed a housekeeper she did the housework and that was all.

Then she went to sit on the front porch, to sew or read a book. 'What nonsense! You get me a good German girl, strong and pretty good-looking. I'll send the money and she can come over here and be my wife,' he wrote.

The letter had been sent to a friend of his young manhood, now a small merchant in a German town, and after talking the matter over with his wife the merchant decided to send his daughter, a woman of twenty-four. She had been engaged to marry a man who was taken sick and had died while he was serving his term in the army, and her father decided she had been mooning about long enough. The merchant called the daughter into a room where he and his wife sat and told her of his decision and, for a long time, she sat looking at the floor. Was she about to make a fuss? A prosperous American husband who owned a big farm was not to be sneezed at. The daughter put up her hand and fumbled with her black hair – there was a great mass of it. After all, she was a big strong woman. Her husband wouldn't be cheated. 'Yes, I'll go,' she said quietly, and getting up walked out of the room.

In America the woman had turned out all right, but her

husband thought her a little too silent. Even though the main purpose in life be to do the work of a house and farm, feed the stock and keep a man's clothes in order, so that he is not always having to buy new ones, still there are times when something else is in order. As he worked in his fields the farmer sometimes muttered to himself. 'Everything in its place. For everything there is a time and a place,' he told himself. One worked and then the time came when one played a little, too. Now and then it was nice to have a few friends about, drink beer, eat a good deal of heavy food and then have some fun, in a kind of way. One did not go too far, but if there were women in the party some-one tickled one of them and she giggled. One made a remark about legs – nothing out of the way. 'Legs is legs. On horses or women legs count a good deal.' Everyone laughed. One had a jolly evening, one had some fun.

Often, after his woman came, the farmer, working in his fields, tried to think what was the matter with her. She worked all the time and the house was in order. Well, she fed the stock so that he did not have to bother about that. What a good cook she was. She even made beer, in the old-fashioned German way, at home – and that was fine, too.

The whole trouble lay in the fact that she was silent, too silent. When one spoke to her she answered nicely but she herself made no conversation, and at night she lay in the bed silently. The German wondered if she would be showing signs of having a child pretty soon. 'That might make a difference,' he thought. He stopped working and looked across the fields to where there was a meadow. His cattle were there feeding quietly. 'Even cows, and surely cows were quiet and silent enough things, even cows had times.

Sometimes the very devil got into a cow. You were leading her along a road or a lane and suddenly she went half
insane. If one weren't careful she would jam her head
through fences, knock a man over, do almost anything.
She wanted something insanely, with a riotous hunger.
Even a cow wasn't always just passive and quiet.' The
German felt cheated. He thought of the friend in Germany who had sent his daughter. 'Ugh, the deuce, he
might have sent a livelier one,' he thought.

It was June when Tom came to the farm and the
harvest was on. The German had planted several large
fields to wheat and the yield was good. Another man had
been employed to work on the farm all summer but Tom
could be used, too. He would have to sleep on the hay in
the barn, but that he did not mind. He went to work at
once.

And anyone knowing Tom, and seeing his huge and
rather ungainly body, must realize that, in his youth, he
might have been unusually strong. For one thing he had
not done so much thinking as he must have done later, nor
had he been for years seated at a desk. He worked in the
fields with the other two men and at the mealtime came
into the house with them to eat. He and the German's
wife must have been a good deal alike. Tom had in his
mind certain things – thoughts concerning his boyhood –
and he was thinking a good deal of the future. Well,
there he was working his way westward and making a little
money all the time as he went, and every cent he made he
kept. He had not yet been into an American city, had
purposely avoided such places as Springfield, Dayton and
Cincinnatti and had kept to the smaller places and the
farms.

After a time he would have an accumulation of money and would go into cities, study, read books, live. He had then a kind of illusion about American cities. 'A city was a great gathering of people who had grown tired of lone-liness and isolation. They had come to realize that only by working together could they have the better things of life. Many hands working together might build wonder-fully, many minds working together might think clearly, many impulses working together might channel all lives into an expression of something rather fine.'

I am making a mistake if I give you the impression that Tom, the boy from the Ohio farm, had any such definite notions. He had a feeling – of a sort. There was a dumb kind of hope in him. He had even then, I am quite sure, something else, that he later always retained, a kind of almost holy inner modesty. It was his chief attraction as a man, but perhaps it stood in the way of his ever achieving the kind of outstanding and assertive manhood we Ameri-cans all seem to think we value so highly.

At any rate, there he was, and there was that woman, the silent one, now twenty-seven years old. The three men sat at table eating and she waited on them. They ate in the farm kitchen, a large old-fashioned one, and she stood by the stove or went silently about putting more food on the table as it was consumed.

At night the men did not eat until late and sometimes darkness came as they sat at table and then she brought lighted lamps for them. Great winged insects flew violently against the screen door and a few moths, that had managed to get into the house, flew about the lamps. When the men had finished eating they sat at the table drinking beer and the woman washed the dishes.

The farm-hand, employed for the summer, was a man of thirty-five, a large bony man with a drooping moustache. He and the German talked. Well, it was good, the German thought, to have the silence of his house broken. The two men spoke of the coming threshing-time and of the hay harvest just completed. One of the cows would be calving next week. Her time was almost here. The man with the moustache took a drink of beer and wiped his moustache with the back of his hand, that was covered with long black hair.

Tom had drawn his chair back against the wall and sat in silence and, when the German was deeply engaged in conversation, he looked at the woman, who sometimes turned from her dish-washing to look at him.

There was something, a certain feeling he had sometimes — she, it might be, also had — but of the two men in the room that could not be said. It was too bad she spoke no English. Perhaps, however, even though she spoke his language, he could not speak to her of the things he meant. But, pshaw! there wasn't anything in his mind, nothing that could be said in words. Now and then her husband spoke to her in German and she replied quietly, and then the conversation between the two men was resumed in English. More beer was brought. The German felt expansive. How good to have talk in the house. He urged beer upon Tom, who took it and drank. 'You're another close-mouthed one, eh?' he said, laughing.

Tom's adventure happened during the second week of his stay. All the people about the place had gone to sleep for the night but, as he could not sleep, he arose silently and came down out of the hay-loft carrying his blanket. It was a silent, hot, soft night without a moon and he went to where there was a small grass plot that came down to the barn, and spreading his blanket sat with his back to the wall of the barn.

That he could not sleep did not matter. He was young and strong. 'If I do not sleep to-night I will sleep to-morrow night,' he thought. There was something in the air that he thought concerned only himself, and that made him want to be thus awake, sitting out of doors and looking at the dim distant trees in the apple orchard near the barn, at the stars in the sky, at the farm-house, faintly seen some few hundred feet away. Now that he was out of doors he no longer felt restless. Perhaps it was only that he was nearer something that was like himself at the moment, just the night perhaps.

He became aware of something, of something moving restlessly in the darkness. There was a fence between the farm-yard and the orchard, with berry bushes growing beside it, and something was moving in the darkness along the berry bushes. Was it a cow that had got out of the stable or were the bushes moved by a wind? He did a trick known to country boys. Thrusting a finger into his mouth he stood up and put the wet finger out before him. A wind would dry one side of the warm wet finger quickly and that side would turn cold. Thus one told oneself something, not only of the strength of a wind but its direction. Well, there was no wind strong enough to move berry bushes – there was no wind at all. He had come down out of the barn loft in his bare feet and in moving about had made no sound, and now he went and stood silently on the blanket with his back against the wall of the barn.

The movement among the bushes was growing more

distinct; but it wasn't in the bushes. Something was moving along the fence, between him and the orchard. There was a place along the fence, an old rail one, where no bushes grew and now the silent, moving thing was passing the open space.

It was the woman of the house, the German's wife. What was up? Was she also trying dumbly to draw nearer something that was like herself, that she could understand, a little? Thoughts flitted through Tom's head and a dumb kind of desire arose within him. He began hoping vaguely that the woman was in search of himself.

Later, when he told me of the happenings of that night, he was quite sure that the feeling that then possessed him was not physical desire for a woman. His own mother had died several years before, and the woman his father had later married had seemed to him just a thing about the house, a not very competent thing, bones, a hank of hair, a body that did not do very well what one's body was supposed to do. 'I was intolerant as the devil, about all women. Maybe I always have been, but then — I'm sure I was a queer kind of country bumpkin aristocrat. I thought myself something, a special thing in the world, and that woman, any women I had ever seen or known, the wives of a few neighbours as poor as my father, a few country girls — I had thought them all beneath my contempt, dirt under my feet.

'About that German's wife I had not felt that way. I don't know why. Perhaps because she had a habit of keeping her mouth shut as I did just at that time, a habit I have since lost.'

And so Tom stood there — waiting. The woman came slowly along the fence, keeping in the shadow of the bushes and then crossed an open space toward the barn.

Now she was walking slowly along the barn wall, directly toward the young man who stood in the heavy shadows holding his breath and waiting for her coming.

Afterward, when he thought of what had happened, he could never quite make up his mind whether she was walking in sleep or was awake as she came slowly toward him. They did not speak the same language and they never saw each other after that night. Perhaps she had only been restless and had got out of the bed beside her husband and made her way out of the house, without any conscious knowledge of what she was doing.

She became conscious when she came to where he was standing, however, conscious and frightened. He stepped out toward her and she stopped. Their faces were very close together and her eyes were large with alarm. 'The pupils dilated,' he said in speaking of that moment. He insisted upon the eyes. 'There was a fluttering something in them. I am sure I do not exaggerate when I say that at the moment I saw everything as clearly as though we had been standing together in the broad daylight. Perhaps something had happened to my own eyes, eh? That might be possible. I could not speak to her, reassure her — I could not say, "Do not be frightened, woman." I couldn't say anything. My eyes, I suppose, had to do all the saying.'

Evidently there was something to be said. At any rate, there my friend stood, on that remarkable night of his youth, and his face and the woman's face drew nearer each other. Then their lips met and he took her into his arms and held her for a moment.

That was all. They stood together, the woman of twenty-seven and the young man of nineteen and he was a country boy and was afraid. That may be the explanation of the fact that nothing else happened.

I do not know as to that, but in telling this tale I have an advantage you who read cannot have. I heard the tale told, brokenly, by the man — who had the experience I am trying to describe. Story-tellers of old times, who went from place to place telling their wonder tales, had an advantage we, who have come in the age of the printed word, do not have. They were both story-tellers and actors. As they talked they modulated their voices, made gestures with their hands. Often they carried conviction simply by the power of their own conviction. All of our modern fussing with style in writing is an attempt to do the same thing.

And what I am trying to express now is a sense I had that night, as my friend talked to me in the park, of a union of two people that took place in the heavy shadows by a barn in Ohio, a union of two people that was not personal, that concerned their two bodies and at the same time did not concern their bodies. The thing has to be felt, not understood with the thinking mind.

Anyway, they stood for a few minutes, five minutes, perhaps, with their bodies pressed against the wall of the barn and their hands together, clasped together tightly. Now and then one of them stepped away from the barn and stood for a moment directly facing the other. One might say it was Europe facing America in the darkness by a barn. One might grow fancy and learned and say almost anything, but all I am saying is that they stood as I am describing them, and oddly enough with their faces to the barn

wall — instinctively turning from the house, I presume —
and that now and then one of them stepped out and stood
for a moment facing the other. Their lips did not meet
after the first moment.

The next step was taken. The German awoke in the
house and began calling, and then he appeared at the
kitchen door with a lantern in his hand. It was the lantern,
his carrying of the lantern, that saved the situation for the
wife and my friend. It made a little circle of light outside
of which he could see nothing, but he kept calling his wife,
whose name was Katherine, in a distracted, frightened way.
'Oh, Katherine. Where are you? Oh, Katherine,' he
called.

My friend acted at once. Taking hold of the woman's
hand he ran — making no sound — along the shadows of the
barn and across the open space between the barn and the
fence. The two people were two dim shadows flitting
along the dark wall of the barn, nothing more, and at the
place in the fence where there were no bushes he lifted her
over and climbed over after her. Then he ran through the
orchard and into the road before the house and putting his
two hands on her shoulders shook her. As though understanding his wish, she answered her husband's call and as
the lantern came swinging down toward them my friend
dodged back into the orchard.

The man and wife went toward the house, the German
talking vigorously and the woman answering quietly, as
she had always answered him. Tom was puzzled. Everything that happened to him that night puzzled him then and
long afterward when he told me of it. Later he worked out
a kind of explanation of it — as all men will do in such cases
— but that is another story and the time to tell it is not now.

The point is that my friend had, at the moment, the feeling of having completely possessed the woman, and with that knowledge came also the knowledge that her husband would never possess her, could never by any chance possess her. A great tenderness swept over him and he had but one desire: to protect the woman, not to by any chance make the life she had yet to live any harder.

And so he ran quickly to the barn, secured the blanket and climbed silently up into the loft.

The farm-hand with the drooping moustache was sleeping quietly on the hay and Tom lay down beside him and closed his eyes. As he expected, the German came, almost at once, to the loft and flashed the lantern, not into the face of the older man but into Tom's face. Then he went away and Tom lay awake smiling happily. He was young then and there was something proud and revengeful in him – in his attitude toward the German, at the moment. 'Her husband knew, but at the same time did not know, that I had taken his woman from him,' he said to me when he told of the incident long afterward. 'I don't know why that made me so happy then, but it did. At the moment I thought I was happy only because we had both managed to escape, but now I know that wasn't it.'

And it is quite sure my friend did have a sense of something. On the next morning when he went into the house the breakfast was on the table, but the woman was not on hand to serve it. The food was on the table and the coffee on the stove and the three men ate in silence. And then Tom and the German stepped out of the house together, stepped, as by a prearranged plan into the barnyard. The German knew nothing – his wife had grown restless in the night and had got out of bed and walked out into the road and both the other men were asleep in the barn. He had never had any reason for suspecting her of anything at all and she was just the kind of woman he had wanted, never went trapsing off to town, didn't spend a lot of money on clothes, was willing to do any kind of work, made no trouble. He wondered why he had taken such a sudden and violent dislike for his young employee.

Tom spoke first. 'I think I'll quit. I think I'd better be on my way,' he said. It was obvious his going, at just that time, would upset the plans the German had made for getting the work done at the rush time; but he made no objection to Tom's going and at once. Tom had arranged to work by the week and the German counted back to the Saturday before and tried to cheat a little. 'I owe you for only one week, eh?' he said. One might as well get two days' extra work out of the man without pay – if it were possible.

But Tom did not intend being defeated. 'A week and four days,' he replied, purposely adding an extra day. 'If you do not want to pay for the four days I'll stay out the week.'

The German went into the house and got the money and Tom set off along the road.

When he had walked for two or three miles he stopped and went into a wood where he stayed all that day thinking of what had happened.

Perhaps he did not do much thinking. What he said, when he told the story that night in the Chicago park, was that all day there were certain figures marching through his mind and that he just sat down on a log and let them march. Did he have some notion that an impulse toward life in himself had come, and that it would not come again?

As he sat on the log there were the figures of his father and his dead mother and of several other people who had lived about the Ohio countryside where he had spent his boyhood. They kept doing things, saying things. It will be quite clear to my readers that I think my friend a story-teller who for some reason has never been able to get his stories outside himself, as one might say, and that might of course explain the day in the wood. He himself thought he was in a sort of comatose state. He had not slept during the night before and, although he did not say as much, there was something a bit mysterious in the thing that had hap-pened to him.

There was one thing he told me concerning that day of dreams that is curious. There appeared in his fancy, over and over again, the figure of a woman he had never seen in the flesh and has never seen since. At any rate, it wasn't the German's wife, he declared.

'The figure was that of a woman, but I could not tell her age,' he said. 'She was walking away from me and was clad in a blue dress covered with black dots. Her figure was slender and looked strong but broken. That's it. She was walking in a path in a country such as I had then never seen, have never seen, a country of very low hills and with-out trees. There was no grass either but only low bushes that came up to her knees. One might have thought it an Arctic country, where there is summer but for a few weeks each year. She had her sleeves rolled to her shoulders so that her slender arms showed, and had buried her face in the crook of her right arm. Her left arm hung like a broken thing, her legs were like broken things, her body was a broken thing.

'And yet, you see, she kept walking and walking, in the

path, among the low bushes, over the barren little hills. She walked vigorously, too. It seems impossible and a foolish thing to tell about, but all day I sat in the woods on the stump, and every time I closed my eyes I saw that woman walking thus, fairly rushing along, and yet, you see, she was all broken to pieces.'

THE MAN WHO BECAME A WOMAN

*

MY father was a retail druggist in our town, out in Nebraska, which was so much like a thousand other towns I've been in since that there's no use fooling around and taking up your time and mine trying to describe it.

Anyway, I became a drug clerk and after father's death the store was sold and mother took the money and went west, to her sister in California, giving me four hundred dollars with which to make my start in the world. I was only nineteen years old then.

I came to Chicago, where I worked as a drug clerk for a time, and then, as my health suddenly went back on me, perhaps because I was so sick of my lonely life in the city and of the sight and smell of the drug store, I decided to set out on what seemed to me then the great adventure, and became for a time a tramp, working now and then, when I had no money, but spending all the time I could loafing around out of doors or riding up and down the land on freight trains and trying to see the world. I even did some stealing in lonely towns at night – once a pretty good suit of clothes that someone had left hanging out on a clothes-line, and once some shoes out of a box in a freight car – but I was in constant terror of being caught and put into jail, so realized that success as a thief was not for me.

The most delightful experience of that period of my life was when I once worked as a groom, or swipe, with race-horses and it was during that time I met a young fellow of about my own age who has since become a writer of some prominence.

The young man of whom I now speak had gone into

race-track work as a groom, to bring a kind of flourish, a high spot, he used to say, into his life.

He was then unmarried and had not been successful as a writer. What I mean is he was free and I guess, with him as with me, there was something he liked about the people who hang about a race-track, the touts, swipes, drivers, niggers and gamblers. You know what a gaudy undependable lot they are — if you've ever been around the tracks much — about the best liars I've ever seen, and not saving money or thinking about morals, like most druggists, drygoods merchants and the others who used to be my father's friends in our Nebraska town — and not bending the knee much either, or kowtowing to people they thought must be grander or richer or more powerful than themselves.

What I mean is, they were an independent, go-to-the-devil, come-have-a-drink-of-whisky kind of a crew and when one of them won a bet, 'knocked 'em off,' we called it, his money was just dirt to him while it lasted. No king or president or soap manufacturer — gone on a trip with his family to Europe — could throw on more dog than one of them, with his big diamond rings and the diamond horseshoe stuck in his necktie and all.

I liked the whole blamed lot pretty well and he did, too.

He was groom temporarily for a pacing gelding named Lumpy Joe owned by a tall black-moustached man named Alfred Kreymborg and trying the best he could to make the bluff to himself he was a real one. It happened that we were on the same circuit, doing the West Pennsylvania county fairs all that fall, and on fine evenings we spent a good deal of time walking and talking together.

Let us suppose it to be a Monday or Tuesday evening and our horses had been put away for the night. The racing didn't start until later in the week, maybe Wednesday, usually. There was always a little place called a dining-hall, run mostly by the Women's Christian Temperance Associations of the towns, and we would go there to eat, where we could get a pretty good meal for twenty-five cents. At least then we thought it pretty good.

I would manage it so that I sat beside this fellow, whose name was Tom Means, and when we had got through eating we would go look at our two horses again and when we got there Lumpy Joe would be eating his hay in his box-stall and Alfred Kreymborg would be standing there, pulling his moustache and looking as sad as a sick crane.

But he wasn't really sad. 'You two boys want to go down-town to see the girls. I'm an old duffer and way past that myself. You go on along. I'll be setting here, anyway, and I'll keep an eye on both the horses for you,' he would say.

So we would set off, going, not into the town to try to get in with some of the town girls, who might have taken up with us because we were strangers and race-track fellows, but out into the country. Sometimes we got into a hilly country and there was a moon. The leaves were falling off the trees and lay in the road so that we kicked them up with the dust as we went along.

To tell the truth I suppose I got to love Tom Means, who was five years older than me, although I wouldn't have dared say so, then. Americans are shy and timid about saying things like that and a man here don't dare own up he loves another man, I've found out, and they are afraid to admit such feelings to themselves even. I guess they're afraid it may be taken to mean something it don't need to at all.

Anyway, we walked along and some of the trees were already bare and looked like people standing solemnly beside the road and listening to what we had to say. Only I didn't say much. Tom Means did most of the talking.

Sometimes we came back to the race-track and it was late and the moon had gone down and it was dark. Then we often walked round and round the track, sometimes a dozen times, before we crawled into the hay to go to bed.

Tom talked always on two subjects, writing and race-horses, but mostly about race-horses. The quiet sounds about the race-tracks and the smells of horses, and the things that go with horses, seemed to get him all excited. 'Oh, hell, Herman Dudley,' he would burst out suddenly, 'don't go talking to me. I know what I think. I've been around more than you have and I've seen a world of people. There isn't any man or woman, not even a fellow's own mother, as fine as a horse, that is to say a thoroughbred horse.'

Sometimes he would go on like that a long time, speaking of people he had seen and their characteristics. He wanted to be a writer later, and what he said was that when he came to be one he wanted to write the way a well-bred horse runs or trots or paces. Whether he ever did it or not I can't say. He has written a lot, but I'm not too good a judge of such things. Anyway, I don't think he has.

But when he got on the subject of horses he certainly was a darby. I would never have felt the way I finally got to feel about horses or enjoyed my stay among them half so much if it hadn't been for him. Often he would go on talking for an hour, maybe, speaking of horses' bodies and of their minds and wills as though they were human beings.

'Lord help us, Herman,' he would say, grabbing hold of my arm, 'don't it get you up in the throat? I say now, when a good one, like that Lumpy Joe I'm swiping, flattens himself at the head of the stretch and he's coming, and you know he's coming, and you know his heart's sound, and he's game, and you know he isn't going to let himself get licked – don't it get you, Herman, don't it get you like the old Harry?'

That's the way he would talk, and then later, sometimes, he'd talk about writing and get himself all het up about that, too. He had some notions about writing I've never got myself around to thinking much about, but just the same maybe his talk, working in me, has led me to want to begin to write this story myself.

There was one experience of that time on the tracks that I am forced, by some feeling inside myself, to tell.

Well, I don't know why but I've just got to. It will be kind of like confession is, I suppose, to a good Catholic, or maybe, better yet, like cleaning up the room you live in, if you are a bachelor, like I was for so long. The room gets pretty mussy and the bed not made some days and clothes and things thrown on the closet floor and maybe under the bed. And then you clean all up and put on new sheets, and then you take off all your clothes and get down on your hands and knees, and scrub the floor so clean you could eat bread off it, and then take a walk and come home after awhile and your room smells sweet and you feel sweetened up and better inside yourself, too.

What I mean is, this story has been on my chest, and I've often dreamed about the happenings in it, even after I married Jessie and was happy. Sometimes I even screamed out at night and so I said to myself, 'I'll write the dang story,' and here goes.

Fall had come on and in the mornings now when we crept out of our blankets, spread out on the hay in the tiny lofts above the horse-stalls, and put our heads out to look around, there was a white rime of frost on the ground. When we woke the horses woke, too. You know how it is at the tracks – the little barn-like stalls with the tiny lofts above are all set along in a row and there are two doors to each stall, one coming up to a horse's breast and then a top one, that is only closed at night and in bad weather.

In the mornings the upper door is swung open and fastened back and the horses put their heads out. There is the white rime on the grass over inside the grey oval the track makes. Usually there is some outfit that has six, ten or even twelve horses, and perhaps they have a negro cook who does his cooking at an open fire in the clear space before the row of stalls, and he is at work now, and the horses with their big fine eyes are looking about and whinnying, and a stallion looks out at the door of one of the stalls and sees a sweet-eyed mare looking at him and sends up his trumpet-call, and a man's voice laughs, and there are no women anywhere in sight or no sign of one anywhere, and everyone feels like laughing and usually does.

It's pretty fine, but I didn't know how fine it was until I got to know Tom Means and heard him talk about it all.

At the time the thing happened of which I am trying to tell now Tom was no longer with me. A week before his owner, Alfred Kreymborg, had taken his horse Lumpy Joe over into the Ohio Fair Circuit and I saw no more of Tom at the tracks.

There was a story going about the stalls that Lumpy Joe,

a big rangy brown gelding, wasn't really named Lumpy Joe at all, that he was a ringer who had made a fast record out in Iowa and up through the north-west country the year before, and that Kreymborg had picked him up and had kept him under wraps all winter and had brought him over into the Pennsylvania country under this new name and made a clean-up in the books.

I know nothing about that and never talked to Tom about it, but anyway, he, Lumpy Joe and Kreymborg were all gone now.

I suppose I'll always remember those days, and Tom's talk at night, and before that in the early September evenings how we sat around in front of the stalls, and Kreymborg sitting on an upturned feed-box and pulling at his long black moustache and sometimes humming a little ditty one couldn't catch the words of. It was something about a deep well and a little grey squirrel crawling up the sides of it, and he never laughed or smiled much but there was something in his solemn grey eyes, not quite a twinkle, something more delicate than that.

The others talked in low tones and Tom and I sat in silence. He never did his best talking except when he and I were alone.

For his sake – if he ever sees my story – I should mention that at the only big track we ever visited, at Readville, Pennsylvania, we saw old Pop Geers, the great racing driver, himself. His horses were at a place far away across the tracks from where we were stabled. I suppose a man like him was likely to get the choice of all the good places for his horses.

We went over there one evening and stood about and there was Geers himself, sitting before one of the stalls on a box tapping the ground with a riding-whip. They called him, around the tracks, 'The silent man from Tennessee,' and he was silent – that night, anyway. All we did was to stand and look at him for maybe a half-hour and then we went away and that night Tom talked better than I had ever heard him. He said that the ambition of his life was to wait until Pop Geers died and then write a book about him, and to show in the book that there was at least one American who never went nutty about getting rich or owning a big factory or being any other kind of a hell of a fellow. 'He's satisfied I think to sit around like that and wait until the big moments of his life come, when he heads a fast one into the stretch and then, darn his soul, he can give all of himself to the thing right in front of him,' Tom said, and then he was so worked up he began to blubber. We were walking along the fence on the inside of the tracks and it was dusk and, in some trees near by, some birds, just sparrows maybe, were making a chirping sound, and you could hear insects singing and, where there was a little light, off to the west between some trees, motes were dancing in the air. Tom said that about Pop Geers, although I think he was thinking most about something he wanted to be himself and wasn't, and then he went and stood by the fence and sort of blubbered and I began to blubber, too, although I didn't know what about.

But perhaps I did know, after all. I suppose Tom wanted to feel, when he became a writer, like he thought old Pop must feel when his horse swung around the upper turn, and there lay the stretch before him, and if he was going to get his horse home in front he had to do it right then. What Tom said was that any man had something in him that understands about a thing like that, but that no woman ever did except up in her brain. He often got off things like that about women, but I notice he later married one of them just the same.

But to get back to my knitting. After Tom had left, the stable I was with kept drifting along through nice little Pennsylvania county seat towns. My owner, a strange excitable kind of a man from over in Ohio, who had lost a lot of money on horses but was always thinking he would maybe get it all back in some big killing, had been playing in pretty good luck that year. The horse I had, a tough little gelding, a five-year-old, had been getting home in front pretty regular and so he took some of his winnings and bought a three-year-old black pacing stallion named 'O, My Man.' My gelding was called 'Pick-it-boy,' because when he was in a race and had got into the stretch my owner always got half wild with excitement and shouted so you could hear him a mile and a half. 'Go, pick it boy, pick it boy, pick it boy,' he kept shouting, and so when he had got hold of this good little gelding he had named him that.

The gelding was a fast one, all right. As the boys at the tracks used to say, he 'picked 'em up sharp and set 'em down clean,' and he was what we called a natural race-horse, right up to all the speed he had, and didn't require much training. 'All you got to do is to drop him down on the track and he'll go,' was what my owner was always saying to other men, when he was bragging about his horse.

And so you see, after Tom left, I hadn't much to do evenings, and then the new stallion, the three-year-old, came on with a negro swipe named Burt.

I liked him fine and he liked me, but not the same as Tom and me. We got to be friends all right, and I suppose

Burt would have done things for me, and maybe me for him, that Tom and me wouldn't have done for each other.

But with a negro you couldn't be close friends like you can with another white man. There's some reason you can't understand, but it's true. There's been too much talk about the difference between whites and blacks and you're both shy, and, anyway, no use trying, and I suppose Burt and I both knew it and so I was pretty lonesome.

Something happened to me that happened several times, when I was a young fellow, that I have never exactly understood. Sometimes now I think it was all because I had got to be almost a man and had never been with a woman. I don't know what's the matter with me. I can't ask a woman. I've tried it a good many times in my life, but every time I've tried the same thing happened.

Of course, with Jessie now, it's different, but at the time of which I'm speaking Jessie was a long ways off and a good many things were to happen to me before I got to her.

Around a race-track, as you may suppose, the fellows who are swipes and drivers and strangers in the towns do not go without women. They don't have to. In any town there are always some fly girls will come around a place like that. I suppose they think they are fooling with men who lead romantic lives. Such girls will come along by the front of the stalls where the race-horses are and, if you look all right to them, they will stop and make a fuss over your horse. They rub their little hands over the horse's nose, and then is the time for you – if you aren't a fellow like me who can't get up the nerve – then is the time for you to smile and say, 'Hello, kid,' and make a date with one of them for that evening up town after supper. I couldn't do that, although the Lord knows I tried hard enough, often enough. A girl would come along alone, and she would be a little thing and give me the eye, and I would try and try but couldn't say anything. Both Tom, and Burt afterwards, used to laugh at me about it sometimes, but what I think is that, had I been able to speak up to one of them and had managed to make a date with her, nothing would have come of it. We would probably have walked around the town and got off together in the dark somewhere, where the town came to an end, and then she would have had to knock me over with a club before it got any further.

And so there I was, having got used to Tom and our talks together, and Burt of course had his own friends among the black men. I got lazy and mopy and had a hard time doing my work.

It was like this. Sometimes I would be sitting, perhaps under a tree, in the late afternoon when the races were over for the day and the crowds had gone away. There were always a lot of other men and boys who hadn't any horses in the races that day, and they would be standing or sitting about in front of the stalls and talking.

I would listen for a time to their talk and then their voices would seem to go far away. The things I was looking at would go far away, too. Perhaps there would be a tree, not more than a hundred yards away, and it would just come out of the ground and float away like a thistle. It would get smaller and smaller, away off there in the sky, and then suddenly – bang, it would be back where it belonged, in the ground, and I would begin hearing the voices of the men talking again.

When Tom was with me that summer the nights were splendid. We usually walked about and talked until pretty late, and then I crawled up into my hole and went to sleep.

Always out of Tom's talk I got something that stayed in my mind, after I was off by myself, curled up in my blanket. I suppose he had a way of making pictures as he talked, and the pictures stayed by me as Burt was always saying pork chops did by him. 'Give me the old pork chops, they stick to the ribs,' Burt was always saying, and with the imagination it was always that way about Tom's talks. He started something inside you that went on and on, and your mind played with it like walking about in a strange town and seeing the sights, and you slipped off to sleep and had splendid dreams and woke up in the morning feeling fine.

And then he was gone and it wasn't that way any more, and I got into the fix I have described. At night I kept seeing women's bodies and women's lips and things in my dreams, and woke up in the morning feeling like the old Harry.

Burt was pretty good to me. He always helped me cool Pick-it-boy out after a race, and he did the things himself that take the most skill and quickness, like getting the bandages on a horse's leg smooth, and seeing that every strap is setting just right, and every buckle drawn up to just the right hole, before your horse goes out on the track for a heat.

Burt knew there was something wrong with me and put himself out not to let the boss know. When the boss was around he was always bragging about me. 'The brightest kid I've ever worked with around the tracks,' he would say, and grin, and that at a time when I wasn't worth my salt.

When you go out with the horses there is one job that always takes a lot of time. In the late afternoon, after your horse has been in a race, and after you have washed him and rubbed him out, he has to be walked slowly, sometimes for hours and hours, so he'll cool out slowly and won't get muscle-bound. I got so I did that job for both our horses and Burt did the more important things. It left him free to go talk or shoot dice with the other niggers, and I didn't mind. I rather liked it, and after a hard race even the stallion, O My Man, was tame enough, even when there were mares about.

You walk and walk and walk, around a little circle, and your horse's head is right by your shoulder, and all around you the life of the place you are in is going on, and in a queer way you get so you aren't really a part of it at all. Perhaps no one ever gets as I was then, except boys that aren't quite men yet and who, like me, have never been with girls or women – to really be with them, up to the hilt, I mean. I used to wonder if young girls got that way, too, before they married or did what we used to call 'go on the town.'

If I remember it right, though, I didn't do much thinking then. Often I would have forgotten supper if Burt hadn't shouted at me and reminded me, and sometimes he forgot and went off to town with one of the other niggers and I did forget.

There I was with the horse, going slow, slow, slow, around a circle that way. The people were leaving the fair-grounds now, some afoot, some driving away to the farms in wagons and Fords. Clouds of dust floated in the air, and over to the west, where the town was, maybe the sun was going down, a red ball of fire through the dust. Only a few hours before the crowd had been all filled with excitement and everyone shouting. Let us suppose my horse had been in a race that afternoon and I had stood in front of the grand-stand with my horse-blanket over my shoulder, alongside of Burt, perhaps, and when they came into the stretch my owner began to call, in that queer high voice of his that seemed to float over the top of all the shouting up in the grand-stand. And his voice was saying over and over, 'Go, pick it boy, pick it boy, pick it boy,' the way he always did, and my heart was thumping so I could hardly breathe, and Burt was leaning over and snapping his fingers and muttering, 'Come, little sweet. Come on home. Your Mama wants you. Come get your 'lasses and bread, little Pick-it-boy.'

Well, all that was over now and the voices of the people left around were all low. And Pick-it-boy – I was leading him slowly around the little ring, to cool him out slowly, as I've said – he was different, too. Maybe he had pretty nearly broken his heart trying to get down to the wire in front, or getting down there in front, and now everything inside him was quiet and tired, as it was nearly all the time those days in me, except in me tired but not quiet.

You remember I've told you we always walked in a circle, round and round and round. I guess something inside me got to going round and round and round, too. The sun did sometimes, and the trees and the clouds of dust. I had to think sometimes about putting down my feet so they went down in the right place and I didn't get to staggering like a drunken man.

And a funny feeling came that it is going to be hard to describe. It had something to do with the life in the horse and in me. Sometimes, these late years, I've thought maybe negroes would understand what I'm trying to talk about now better than any white man ever will. I mean something about men and animals, something between them, something that can perhaps only happen to a white man when he has slipped off his base a little, as I suppose I had then. I think maybe a lot of horsy people feel it some-times, though. It's something like this, maybe – do you suppose it could be that something we whites have got, and think such a lot of, and are so proud about, isn't much of any good after all?

It's something in us that wants to be big and grand and important, maybe, and won't let us just be, like a horse or a dog or a bird can. Let's say Pick-it-boy had won his race that day. He did that pretty often that summer. Well, he was neither proud, like I would have been in his place, nor mean in one part of the inside of him either. He was just himself, doing something with a kind of simplicity. That's what Pick-it-boy was like, and I got to feeling it in him as I walked with him slowly in the gathering darkness. I got inside him in some way I can't explain and he got inside me. Often we would stop walking for no cause and he would put his nose up against my face.

I wished he was a girl sometimes, or that I was a girl and he was a man. It's an odd thing to say, but it's a fact. Being with him that way, so long, and in such a quiet way, cured something in me a little. Often after an evening like that I slept all right and did not have the kind of dreams I've spoken about.

But I wasn't cured for very long, and couldn't get cured. My body seemed all right and just as good as ever, but there wasn't no pep in me.

Then the fall got later and later and we came to the last town we were going to make before my owner laid his horses up for the winter, in his home-town over across the State line in Ohio, and the track was up on a hill, or rather in a kind of high plain above the town.

It wasn't much of a place, and the sheds were rather rickety and the track bad, especially at the turns. As soon as we got to the place and got stabled it began to rain, and kept it up all week, so the fair had to be put off.

As the purses weren't very large, a lot of the owners shipped right out, but our owner stayed. The fair owners guaranteed expenses, whether the races were held the next week or not.

And all week there wasn't much of anything for Burt and me to do but clean manure out of the stalls in the morning, watch for a chance, when the rain let up a little, to jog the horses around the track in the mud, and then clean them off, blanket them and stick them back in their stalls.

It was the hardest time of all for me. Burt wasn't so bad off, as there were a dozen or two blacks around, and in the evening they went off to town, got liquored up a little, and came home late, singing and talking, even in the cold rain.

And then one night I got mixed up in the thing I'm trying to tell you about.

It was a Saturday evening, and when I look back at it now it seems to me everyone had left the tracks but just me. In the early evening swipe after swipe came over to my stall and asked me if I was going to stick around. When I said I was, he would ask me to keep an eye out for him, that nothing happened to his horse. 'Just take a stroll down that way now and then, eh, kid,' one of them would say, 'I just want to run up to town for an hour or two.'

I would say 'yes' to be sure, and so pretty soon it was dark as pitch up there in that little ruined fair-ground and nothing living anywhere around but the horses and me.

I stood it as long as I could, walking here and there in the mud and rain, and thinking all the time I wished I was someone else and not myself. 'If I were someone else,' I thought, 'I wouldn't be here, but down there in town with the others.' I saw myself going into saloons and having drinks, and later going off to a house, maybe, and getting myself a woman.

I got to thinking so much that, as I went stumbling around up there in the darkness, it was as though what was in my mind was actually happening.

Only I wasn't with some cheap woman, such as I would have found had I had the nerve to do what I wanted, but with such a woman as I thought then I should never find in this world. She was slender and like a flower, and with something in her like a race-horse, too, something in her like Pick-it-boy in the stretch, I guess.

And I thought about her and thought about her until I couldn't stand thinking any more. 'I'll do something, anyway,' I said to myself.

So, although I had told all the swipes I would stay and watch their horses, I went out of the fair-grounds and down the hill a ways. I went down until I came to a little low saloon, not in the main part of the town itself but half-way up the hill-side. The saloon had once been a residence, a farm-house, perhaps; but if it was ever a farm-house, I'm sure the farmer who lived there and worked the land on that hill-side hadn't made out very well. The country didn't look like a farming country, such as one sees all about the other county-seat towns we had been visiting all through the late summer and fall. Everywhere you looked there were stones sticking out of the ground and the trees mostly of the stubby, stunted kind. It looked wild and untidy and ragged, that's what I mean. On the flat plain, up above, where the fair-ground was, there were a few fields and pastures, and there were some sheep raised, and in the field right next to the tracks, on the farthest side from town, on the back stretch side, there had once been a slaughter-house, the ruins of which were still standing. It hadn't been used for quite some time, but there were bones of animals lying all about in the field, and there was a smell coming out of the old building that would curl your hair.

The horses hated the place, just as we swipes did, and in the morning when we were jogging them around the track in the mud, to keep them in racing condition, Pick-it-boy and O My Man both raised old Ned every time we headed them up the back stretch and got near to where the old slaughter-house stood. They would rear and fight at the bit, and go off their stride and run until they got clear of the rotten smells, and neither Burt nor I could make them stop it. 'It's a hell of a town down there, and this is a hell of a track for racing,' Burt kept saying. 'If they ever have their danged old fair someone's going to get spilled, and maybe killed, back here.' Whether they did or not I don't know, as I didn't stay for the fair, for reasons I'll tell you pretty soon; but Burt was speaking sense all right. A race-horse isn't like a human being. He won't stand for it to have to do his work in any rotten ugly kind of a dump the way a man will, and he won't stand for the smells a man will either.

But to get back to my story again. There I was, going down the hill-side in the darkness and the cold, soaking rain and breaking my word to all the others about staying up above and watching the horses. When I got to the little saloon I decided to stop and have a drink or two. I'd found out long before that about two drinks upset me so I was two-thirds piped and couldn't walk straight, but on that night I didn't care a tinker's damn.

So I went up a kind of path, out of the road, toward the front door of the saloon. It was in what must have been the parlour of the place when it was a farm-house, and there was a little front porch.

I stopped before I opened the door and looked about a little. From where I stood I could look right down into the main street of the town, like being in a big city, like New York or Chicago, and looking down out of the fifteenth floor of an office building into the street.

The hill-side was mighty steep and the road up had to wind and wind, or no one could ever have come up out of the town to their plagued old fair at all.

It wasn't much of a town I saw — a main street with a lot of saloons and a few stores, one or two dinky moving-picture places, a few Fords, hardly any women or girls in sight, and a raft of men. I tried to think of the girl I had been dreaming about, as I walked around in the mud and darkness up at the fair-ground, living in the place, but I couldn't make it. It was like trying to think of Pick-it-boy getting himself worked up to the state I was in then, and going into the ugly dump I was going into. It couldn't be done.

All the same, I knew the town wasn't all right there in sight. There must have been a good many of the kinds of houses Pennsylvania miners live in back in the hills, or around a turn in the valley in which the main street stood.

What I suppose is that, it being Saturday night and rain-ing, the women and kids had all stayed at home and only the men were out, intending to get themselves liquored up. I've been in some other mining towns since, and if I was a miner and had to live in one of them, or in one of the houses they live in with their women and kids, I'd get out and liquor myself up, too.

So there I stood looking, and as sick as a dog inside myself, and as wet and cold as a rat in a sewer-pipe. I could see the mass of dark figures moving about down below, and beyond the main street there was a river that made a sound you could hear distinctly, even up where I was, and over beyond the river were some railroad tracks with switch engines going up and down. I suppose they had something to do with the mines in which the men of the town worked. Anyway, as I stood watching and listening there was, now and then, a sound like thunder rolling down the sky, and I suppose that was a lot of coal, maybe a whole carload, being let down plunk into a coal car.

And then besides there was, on the side of a hill far away, a long row of coke-ovens. They had little doors, through which the light from the fire within leaked out, and as they were set closely, side by side, they looked like the teeth of some big man-eating giant lying and waiting over there in the hills.

The sight of it all, even the sight of the kind of hell-holes men are satisfied to go on living in, gave me the fantods and the shivers right down in my liver, and on that night I guess I had in me a kind of contempt for all men, including myself, that I've never had so thoroughly since. Come right down to it, I suppose women aren't so much to blame as men. They aren't running the show.

D

Then I pushed open the door and went into the saloon. There were about a dozen men, miners, I suppose, playing cards at tables in a little long dirty room, with a bar at one side of it, and with a big red-faced man with a moustache standing back of the bar.

The place smelled, as such places do where men hang around who have worked and sweated in their clothes, and perhaps slept in them too, and have never had them washed, but have just kept on wearing them. I guess you know what I mean if you've ever been in a city. You smell that smell in a city, in street cars on rainy nights when a lot of factory hands get on. I got pretty used to that smell when I was a tramp, and pretty sick of it, too.

And so I was in the place now, with a glass of whisky in my hand, and I thought all the miners were staring at me, which they weren't at all; but I thought they were, and so I felt just the same as though they had been. And then I looked up and saw my own face in the old cracked looking-glass back of the bar. If the miners had been staring, or laughing at me, I wouldn't have wondered when I saw what I looked like.

It – I mean my own face – was white and pasty-looking, and for some reason, I can't tell exactly why, it wasn't my own face at all. It's a funny business I'm trying to tell you about, and I know what you may be thinking of me as well as you do, so you needn't suppose I'm innocent or ashamed. I'm only wondering. I've thought about it a lot since and I can't make it out. I know I was never that way before that night, and I know I've never been that way since. Maybe it was lonesomeness, just lonesomeness, gone on in me too long. I've often wondered if women generally are lonesomer than men.

The point is that the face I saw in the looking-glass back of that bar, when I looked up from my glass of whisky that evening, wasn't my own face at all, but the face of a woman. It was a girl's face, that's what I mean. That's what it was. It was a girl's face, and a lonesome and scared girl, too. She was just a kid at that.

When I saw that, the glass of whisky came pretty near falling out of my hand; but I gulped it down, put a dollar on the bar, and called for another. 'I've got to be careful here — I'm up against something new,' I said to myself. 'If any of these men in here get on to me there's going to be trouble.' When I had got the second drink in me I called for a third, and I thought, 'When I get this third drink down I'll get out of here and back up the hill to the fair-ground before I make a fool of myself and begin to get drunk.'

And then, while I was thinking and drinking my third glass of whisky, the men in the room began to laugh, and of course I thought they were laughing at me. But they weren't. No one in the place had really paid any attention to me.

What they were laughing at was a man who had just come in at the door. I'd never seen such a fellow. He was a huge big man, with red hair that stuck straight up like bristles out of his head, and he had a red-haired kid in his arms. The kid was just like himself, big, I mean, for his age, and with the same kind of stiff red hair.

He came and sat the kid up on the bar, close beside me, and called for a glass of whisky for himself, and all the men in the room began to shout and laugh at him and his kid. Only they didn't shout and laugh when he was looking, so he could tell which ones did it, but did all their shouting and laughing when his head was turned the other way. They kept calling him 'cracked.' 'The crack is getting wider in the old tin pan,' someone sang, and then they all laughed.

I'm puzzled, you see, just how to make you feel as I felt that night. I suppose, having undertaken to write this story, that's what I'm up against, trying to do that. I'm not claiming to be able to inform you or to do you any good. I'm just trying to make you understand some things about me, as I would like to understand some things about you, or anyone, if I had the chance. Anyway, the whole blamed thing, the thing that went on, I mean, in that little saloon on that rainy Saturday night, wasn't like anything quite real. I've already told you how I had looked into the glass back of the bar and had seen there, not my own face, but the face of a scared young girl. Well, the men, the miners, sitting at the tables in the half-dark room, the red-faced bartender, the unholy-looking big man who had come in and his queer-looking kid, now sitting on the bar – all of them were like characters in some play, not like real people at all.

There was myself, that wasn't myself – and I'm not any fairy. Anyone who has ever known me knows better than that.

And then there was the man who had come in. There was a feeling came out of him that wasn't like the feeling you get from a man at all. It was more like the feeling you get maybe from a horse, only his eyes weren't like a horse's eyes. Horses' eyes have a kind of calm something in them, and his hadn't. If you've ever carried a lantern through a wood at night, going along a path, and then suddenly you felt something funny in the air and stopped, and there ahead of you somewhere were the eyes of some little animal, gleaming out at you from a dead wall of darkness – The eyes shine big and quiet, but there is a point right in the centre of each where there is something dancing and wavering. You aren't afraid the little animal will jump at you, you are afraid the little eyes will jump at you – that's what's the matter with you.

Only, of course, a horse, when you go into his stall at night, or a little animal you had disturbed in a wood that way, wouldn't be talking, and the big man who had come in there with his kid was talking. He kept talking all the time, saying something under his breath, as they say, and I could only understand now and then a few words. It was his talking made him kind of terrible. His eyes said one thing and his lips another. They didn't seem to get together, as though they belonged to the same person.

For one thing, the man was too big. There was about him an unnatural bigness. It was in his hands, his arms, his shoulders, his body, his head, a bigness like you might see in trees and bushes in a tropical country, perhaps. I've never been in a tropical country, but I've seen pictures. Only his eyes were small. In his big head they looked like the eyes of a bird. And I remember that his lips were thick, like negroes' lips.

He paid no attention to me or to the others in the room, but kept on muttering to himself, or to the kid sitting on the bar – I couldn't tell to which.

First he had one drink and then, quick, another. I stood staring at him and thinking – a jumble of thoughts, I suppose.

What I must have been thinking was something like this. 'Well, he's one of the kind you are always seeing about towns,' I thought. I meant he was one of the cracked kind. In almost any small town you go to you will find one, and sometimes two or three cracked people, walking around. They go through the street, muttering to themselves, and people generally are cruel to them. Their own folks make a bluff at being kind, but they aren't really, and the others in the town, men and boys, like to tease them. They send such a fellow, the mild, silly kind, on some fool errand after a round square or a dozen post-holes, or tie cards on his back saying 'Kick me,' or something like that, and then carry on and laugh as though they had done something funny.

And so there was this cracked one in that saloon, and I could see the men in there wanted to have some fun putting up some kind of horseplay on him, but they didn't quite dare. He wasn't one of the mild kind, that was a cinch. I kept looking at the man and at his kid, and then up at that strange unreal reflection of myself in the cracked looking-glass back of the bar. 'Rats, rats, digging in the ground — miners are rats, little jack-rabbit,' I heard him say to his solemn-faced kid. I guess, after all, maybe he wasn't so cracked.

The kid sitting on the bar kept blinking at his father, like an owl caught out in the daylight, and now the father was having another glass of whisky. He drank six glasses, one right after the other, and it was cheap ten-cent stuff. He must have had cast-iron insides all right.

Of the men in the room, there were two or three (maybe they were really more scared than the others so had to put up a bluff of bravery by showing off) who kept laughing and making funny cracks about the big man and his kid, and there was one fellow was the worst of the bunch.

I'll never forget that fellow because of his looks, and what happened to him afterwards.

He was one of the showing-off kind all right, and he was the one that had started the song about the crack getting bigger in the old tin pan. He sang it two or three times, and then he grew bolder and got up and began walking up and down the room, singing it over and over. He was a showy kind of man with a fancy vest, on which there were brown tobacco spots, and he wore glasses. Every time he made some crack he thought was funny, he winked at the others as though to say, 'You see me. I'm not afraid of this big fellow,' and then the others laughed.

The proprietor of the place must have known what was going on, and the danger in it, because he kept leaning over the bar and saying, 'Shush, now quit it,' to the showy-off man; but it didn't do any good. The fellow kept prancing like a turkey-cock, and he put his hat on one side of his head and stopped right back of the big man and sang that song about the crack in the old tin pan. He was one of the kind you can't shush until they get their blocks knocked off, and it didn't take him long to come to it that time, anyhow.

Because the big fellow just kept on muttering to his kid and drinking his whisky, as though he hadn't heard anything, and then suddenly he turned and his big hand flashed out, and he grabbed, not the fellow who had been showing off, but me. With just a sweep of his arm he brought me up against his big body. Then he shoved me over with my breast jammed against the bar and looking right into his kid's face, and he said, 'Now you watch him, and if you let him fall, I'll kill you,' in just quiet ordinary tones, as though he was saying 'good morning' to some neighbour.

Then the kid leaned over and threw his arms around my head, and in spite of that I did manage to screw my head around enough to see what happened.

It was a sight I'll never forget. The big fellow had whirled around, and he had the showy-off man by the shoulder now, and the fellow's face was a sight. The big man must have had some reputation as a bad man in the town, even though he was cracked, for the man with the fancy vest had his mouth open now, and his hat had fallen off his head, and he was silent and scared. Once, when I was a tramp, I saw a kid killed by a train. The kid was walking on the rail and showing off before some other kids, by letting them see how close he could let an engine come to him before he got out of the way. And the engine was whistling, and a woman, over on the porch of a house near by, was jumping up and down and screaming, and the kid let the engine get nearer and nearer, wanting more and more to show off, and then he stumbled and fell. God! I'll never forget the look on his face, in just the second before he got hit and killed; and now, there in that saloon, was the same terrible look on another face.

I closed my eyes for a moment and was sick all through me, and then, when I opened my eyes, the big man's fist was just coming down in the other man's face. The one blow knocked him cold and he fell down like a beast hit with an axe.

And then the most terrible thing of all happened. The big man had on heavy boots, and he raised one of them and brought it down on the other man's shoulder, as he lay white and groaning on the floor. I could hear the bones crunch, and it made me so sick I could hardly stand up; but I had to stand up and hold on to that kid, or I knew it would be my turn next.

Because the big fellow didn't seem excited or anything, but kept on muttering to himself as he had been doing when he was standing peacefully by the bar drinking his whisky, and now he had raised his foot again, and maybe this time he would bring it down in the other man's face and 'just eliminate his map for keeps,' as sports and prize-fighters sometimes say. I trembled, like I was having a chill, but, thank God, at that moment the kid, who had his arms around me and one hand clinging to my nose, so that there were the marks of his finger-nails on it the next morning, at that moment the kid, thank God, began to howl, and his father didn't bother any more with the man on the floor but turned around, knocked me aside and, taking the kid in his arms, tramped out of that place, muttering to himself as he had been doing ever since he came in.

I went out, too, but I didn't prance out with any dignity, I'll tell you that. I slunk out like a thief or a coward, which perhaps I am, partly, anyhow.

And so there I was, outside there in the darkness, and it was as cold and wet and black and God-forsaken a night as any man ever saw. I was so sick at the thought of human beings that night I could have vomited to think of them at all. For a while I just stumbled along in the mud of the road, going up the hill, back to the fair-ground, and then, almost before I knew where I was, I found myself in the stall with Pick-it-boy.

That was one of the best and sweetest feelings I've ever had in my whole life, being in that warm stall alone with that horse that night. I had told the other swipes that I would go up and down the row of stalls now and then and have an eye on the other horses, but I had altogether forgotten my promise now. I went and stood with my back against the side of the stall, thinking how mean and low and all balled-up and twisted up human beings can become, and how the best of them are likely to get that way any time, just because they are human beings and not simple and clear in their minds, and inside themselves, as animals are, maybe.

Perhaps you know how a person feels at such a moment. There are things you think of, odd little things you had thought you had forgotten. Once, when you were a kid, you were with your father, and he was all dressed up, as for a funeral or Fourth of July, and was walking along a street holding your hand. And you were going past a railroad station, and there was a woman standing. She was a stranger in your town, and was dressed as you had never seen a woman dressed before, and never thought you would see one, looking so nice. Long afterwards you knew that was because she had lovely taste in clothes, such as so few women have really, but then you thought she must be a queen. You had read about queens in fairy stories and the thoughts of them thrilled you. What lovely eyes the strange lady had, and what beautiful rings she wore on her fingers.

Then your father came out from being in the railroad station, maybe to set his watch by the station clock, and took you by the hand, and he and the woman smiled at each other, in an embarrassed kind of way, and you kept looking longingly back at her, and when you were out of her hearing you asked your father if she really were a queen. And it may be that your father was one who wasn't so very hot on democracy and a free country and talked-up bunk about a free citizenry, and he said he hoped she was a queen, and maybe, for all he knew, she was.

Or maybe, when you get jammed up as I was that night, and can't get things clear about yourself or other people, and why you are alive, or for that matter why anyone you can think about is alive, you think, not of people at all, but of other things you have seen and felt — like walking along a road in the snow in the winter, perhaps out in Iowa, and hearing soft warm sounds in a barn close to the road, or of another time when you were on a hill and the sun was going down, and the sky suddenly became a great soft-coloured bowl, all glowing like a jewel-handled bowl, a great queen in some far-away mighty kingdom might have put on a vast table out under the tree, once a year, when she invited all her loyal and loving subjects to come and dine with her.

I can't, of course, figure out what you try to think about when you are as desolate as I was that night. Maybe you are like me and inclined to think of women, and maybe you are like a man I met once, on the road, who told me that when he was up against it he never thought of anything but grub and a big nice clean warm bed to sleep in. 'I don't care about anything else and I don't ever let myself think of anything else,' he said. 'If I was like you, and went to thinking about women, some time I'd find myself hooked up to some skirt, and she'd have the old double cross on me, and the rest of my life maybe I'd be working in some factory for her and her kids.'

As I say, there I was, anyway, up there alone with that horse in that warm stall in that dark, lonesome fair-ground, and I had that feeling about being sick at the thought of human beings and what they could be like.

Well, suddenly I got again the queer feeling I'd had about him once or twice before, I mean the feeling about our understanding each other in some way I can't explain.

So having it again, I went over to where he stood and began running my hands all over his body, just because I loved the feel of him, and as sometimes, to tell the plain truth, I've felt about touching with my hands the body of a woman I've seen and who I thought was lovely too. I ran my hands over his head and neck, and then down over his hard, firm, round body, and then over his flanks and down his legs. His flanks quivered a little, I remember, and once he turned his head and stuck his cold nose down along my neck and nipped my shoulder a little, in a soft, playful way. It hurt a little, but I didn't care.

So then I crawled up through a hole into the loft above, thinking that night was over anyway, and glad of it; but it wasn't, not by a long sight.

As my clothes were all soaking wet, and as we race-track swipes didn't own any such things as night-gowns or pyjamas, I had to go to bed naked, of course.

But we had plenty of horse-blankets, and so I tucked myself in between a pile of them and tried not to think any more that night. The being with Pick-it-boy and having him close right under me that way made me feel a little better.

Then I was sound asleep and dreaming and — bang, like being hit with a club by someone who has sneaked up behind you — I got another wallop.

What I suppose is that, being upset the way I was, I had forgotten to bolt the door to Pick-it-boy's stall down

below, and two negro men had come in there, thinking
they were in their own place, and had climbed up through
the hole where I was. They were half lit-up, but not
what you might call dead-drunk, and I suppose they were
up against something a couple of white swipes, who had
some money in their pockets, wouldn't have been up
against.

What I mean is that a couple of white swipes, having
liquored themselves up and being down there in the town
on a bat, if they wanted a woman or a couple of women
would have been able to find them. There is always a few
women of that kind can be found around any town I've
ever seen or heard of, and of course a bartender would
have given them the tip where to go.

But a negro, up there in that country, where there
aren't any, or anyway mighty few negro women, wouldn't
know what to do when he felt that way and would be up
against it.

It's so always. Burt and several other negroes I've
known pretty well have talked to me about it lots of times.
You take now a young negro man — not a race-track swipe
or a tramp or any other low-down kind of a fellow — but,
let us say, one who has been to college, and has behaved
himself and tried to be a good man, the best he could, and
be clean, as they say. He isn't any better off, is he? If he
has made himself some money and wants to go sit in a swell
restaurant, or go to hear some good music, or see a good
play at the theatre, he gets what we used to call on the
tracks, 'the messy end of the dung-fork,' doesn't he?

And even in such a low-down place as what people call
a 'bad house' it's the same way. The white swipes and
others can go into a place where they have negro women

fast enough, and they do it too; but you let a negro swipe try it the other way around and see how he comes out.

You see, I can think this whole thing out fairly now, sitting here in my own house and writing, and with my wife Jessie in the kitchen, making a pie or something, and I can show just how the two negro men who came into that loft, where I was asleep, were justified in what they did, and I can preach about how the negroes are up against it in this country, like a daisy; but I tell you what, I didn't think things out that way that night.

For, you understand, what they thought, they being half liquored-up, and when one of them had jerked the blankets off me, was that I was a woman. One of them carried a lantern, but it was smoky and dirty and didn't give out much light. So they must have figured it out — my body being pretty white and slender then, like a young girl's body, I suppose — that some white swipe had brought me up there. The kind of girls around a town that will come with a swipe to a race-track on a rainy night aren't very fancy females, but you'll find that kind in the towns all right. I've seen many a one in my day.

And so, I figure, these two big buck niggers, being piped that way, just made up their minds they would snatch me away from the white swipe who had brought me out there, and who had left me lying carelessly around.

'Jes' you lie still, honey. We ain't gwine hurt you none,' one of them said, with a little chuckling laugh that had something in it besides a laugh, too. It was the kind of laugh that gives you the shivers.

The devil of it was I couldn't say anything, not even a word. Why I couldn't yell out and say 'What the hell,' and just kid them a little and shoo them out of there, I don't know, but I couldn't. I tried and tried so that my throat hurt, but I didn't say a word. I just lay there staring at them.

It was a mixed-up night. I've never gone through another night like it.

Was I scared? Lord Almighty, I'll tell you what, I was scared.

Because the two big black faces were leaning right over me now, and I could feel their liquored-up breaths on my cheeks, and their eyes were shining in the dim light from that smoky lantern, and right in the centre of their eyes was that dancing flickering light I've told you about your seeing in the eyes of wild animals when you were carrying a lantern through the woods at night.

It was a puzzler! All my life, you see — me never having had any sisters, and at that time never having had a sweetheart either — I had been dreaming and thinking about women, and I suppose I'd always been dreaming about a pure, innocent one, for myself, made for me by God, maybe. Men are that way. No matter how big they talk about 'let the women go hang,' they've always got that notion tucked away inside themselves, somewhere. It's a kind of chesty man's notion, I suppose, but they've got it, and the kind of up-and-coming women we have nowadays who are always saying, 'I'm as good as a man and will do what the men do,' are on the wrong trail if they really ever want to what you might say 'hog-tie' a fellow of their own.

So I had invented a kind of princess, with black hair and a slender willowy body, to dream about. And I thought of her as being shy and afraid to ever tell anything she really felt to anyone but just me. I suppose I fancied that

III

if I ever found such a woman in the flesh I would be the strong sure one, and she the timid, shrinking one.

And now I was that woman, or something like her, myself.

I gave a kind of wriggle, like a fish you have just taken off the hook. What I did next wasn't a thought-out thing. I was caught, and I squirmed, that's all.

The two niggers both jumped at me, but somehow — the lantern having been kicked over and having gone out the first move they made — well, in some way, when they both lunged at me they missed.

As good luck would have it, my feet found the hole where you put hay down to the horse in the stall below, and through which we crawled up when it was time to go to bed in our blankets up in the hay, and down I slid, not bothering to try to find the ladder with my feet, but just letting myself go.

In less than a second I was out of doors in the dark and the rain, and the two blacks were down the hole and out the door of the stall after me.

How long or how far they really followed me I suppose I'll never know. It was black dark and raining hard now, and a roaring wind had begun to blow. Of course, my body being white, it must have made some kind of a faint streak in the darkness as I ran, and, anyway, I thought they could see me and I knew I couldn't see them, and that made my terror ten times worse. Every minute I thought they would grab me.

You know how it is when a person is all upset and full of terror, as I was. I suppose, maybe, the two niggers followed me for a while, running across the muddy race-track and into the grove of trees that grew in the oval inside the track, but likely enough, after just a few minutes, they gave up the chase and went back, found their own place and went to sleep. They were liquored-up, as I've said, and maybe partly funning too.

But I didn't know that, if they were. As I ran I kept hearing sounds, sounds made by the rain coming down through the dead old leaves left on the trees and by the wind blowing, and it may be that the sound that scared me most of all was my own bare feet stepping on a dead branch and breaking it, or something like that.

There was something strange and scary, a steady sound, like a heavy man running and breathing hard, right at my shoulder. It may have been my own breath, coming quick and fast. And I thought I heard that chuckling laugh I'd heard up in the loft, the laugh that sent the shivers right down through me. Of course, every tree I came close to looked like a man standing there, ready to grab me, and I kept dodging and going – bang – into other trees. My shoulders kept knocking against trees in that way, and the skin was all knocked off, and every time it happened I thought a big black hand had come down and clutched at me and was tearing my flesh.

How long it went on I don't know, maybe an hour, maybe five minutes. But, anyway, the darkness didn't let up, and the terror didn't let up, and I couldn't, to save my life, scream or make any sound.

Just why I couldn't I don't know. Could it be because at the time I was a woman, while at the same time I wasn't a woman? It may be that I was too ashamed of having turned into a girl and being afraid of a man to make any sound. I don't know about that. It's over my head.

But anyway, I couldn't make a sound. I tried and tried and my throat hurt from trying, and no sound came.

And then, after a long time, or what seemed like a long time, I got out from among the trees inside the track and was on the track itself again. I thought the two black men were still after me, you understand, and I ran like a madman.

Of course, running along the track that way – it must have been up the back stretch – I came after a time to where the old slaughter-house stood, in that field beside the track. I knew it by its ungodly smell, scared as I was. Then, in some way, I managed to get over the high old fair-ground fence, and was in the field where the slaughter-house was.

All the time I was trying to yell or scream, or be sensible and tell those two black men that I was a man and not a woman, but I couldn't make it. And then I heard a sound like a board cracking or breaking in the fence, and thought they were still after me.

So I kept on running like a crazy man, in the field, and just then I stumbled and fell over something. I've told you how the old slaughter-house field was filled with bones that had been lying there a long time and had all been washed white. There were heads of sheep and cows and all kinds of things.

And when I fell and pitched forward, I fell right into the midst of something still and cold and white.

It was probably the skeleton of a horse lying there. In small towns like that, they take an old worn-out horse that has died, and haul him off to some field outside of town and skin him for the hide, that they can sell for a dollar or two. It doesn't make any difference what the horse has been, that's the way he usually ends up. Maybe even

Pick-it-boy, or O My Man, or a lot of other good fast ones I've seen and known, have ended that way by this time.

And so I think it was the bones of a horse lying there, and he must have been lying on his back. The birds and wild animals had picked all his flesh away and the rain had washed his bones clean.

Anyway, I fell and pitched forward and my side got cut pretty deep, and my hands clutched at something. I had fallen right in between the ribs of the horse and they seemed to wrap themselves around me close. And my hands, clutching upwards, had got hold of the cheeks of that dead horse, and the bones of his cheeks were cold as ice with the rain washing over them. White bones wrapped around me and white bones in my hands.

There was a new terror now that seemed to go down to the very bottom of me, to the bottom of the inside of me, I mean. It shook me like I have seen a rat in a barn shaken by a dog. It was a terror like a big wave that hits you when you are walking on a seashore, maybe. You see it coming and you try to run and get away, but when you start to run inshore there is a stone cliff you can't climb. So the wave comes high as a mountain, and there it is, right in front of you, and nothing in all this world can stop it. And now it had knocked you down and rolled and tumbled you over and over and washed you clean, clean, but dead, maybe.

And that's the way I felt – I seemed to myself dead with blind terror. It was a feeling like the finger of God running down your back and burning you clean, I mean.

It burned all that silly nonsense about being a girl right out of me.

115

I screamed at last, and the spell that was on me was broken. I'll bet the scream I let out of me could have been heard a mile and a half.

Right away I felt better and crawled out from among the pile of bones, and then I stood on my own feet again, and I wasn't a woman or a young girl any more, but a man and my own self, and as far as I know I've been that way ever since. Even the black night seemed warm and alive now, like a mother might be to a kid in the dark.

Only I couldn't go back to the race-track, because I was blubbering and crying and was ashamed of myself and of what a fool I had made of myself. Someone might see me, and I couldn't stand that, not at that moment.

So I went across the field, walking now, not running like a crazy man, and pretty soon I came to a fence and crawled over and got into another field, in which there was a straw stack, I just happened to find in the pitch darkness.

The straw stack had been there a long time, and some sheep had nibbled away at it until they had made a pretty deep hole, like a cave, in the side of it. I found the hole and crawled in, and there were some sheep in there, about a dozen of them.

When I came in, creeping on my hands and knees, they didn't make much fuss, just stirred around a little and then settled down.

So I settled down amongst them, too. They were warm and gentle and kind, like Pick-it-boy, and being in there with them made me feel better than I would have felt being with any human person I knew at that time.

So I settled down and slept after a while, and when I woke up it was daylight and not very cold, and the rain was over. The clouds were breaking away from the sky now and maybe there would be a fair the next week, but if there was, I knew I wouldn't be there to see it.

Because what I expected to happen did happen. I had to go back across the fields and the fair-ground to the place where my clothes were, right in the broad daylight, and me stark naked, and of course I knew someone would be up and would raise a shout, and every swipe and every driver would stick his head out and would whoop with laughter.

And there would be a thousand questions asked, and I would be too mad and too ashamed to answer, and would perhaps begin to blubber, and that would make me more ashamed than ever.

It all turned out just as I expected, except that when the noise and the shouts of laughter were going it the loudest Burt came out of the stall where O My Man was kept, and when he saw me he didn't know what was the matter, but he knew something was up that wasn't on the square and for which I wasn't to blame.

So he got so all-fired mad he couldn't speak for a minute, and then he grabbed a pitchfork and began prancing up and down before the other stalls, giving that gang of swipes and drivers such a royal old dressing-down as you never heard. You should have heard him sling language. It was grand to hear.

And while he was doing it I sneaked up into the loft, blubbering because I was so pleased and happy to hear him swear that way, and I got my wet clothes on quick and got down, and gave Pick-it-boy a good-bye kiss on the cheek and lit out.

The last I saw of all that part of my life was Burt, still

going it, and yelling out for the man who had put up a trick on me to come out and get what was coming to him. He had the pitchfork in his hand and was swinging it around, and every now and then he would make a kind of lunge at a tree or something, he was so mad through, and there was no one else in sight at all. And Burt didn't even see me cutting out along the fence, through a gate and down the hill and out of the race-horse and the tramp life for the rest of my days.

MILK BOTTLES

*

I LIVED, during that summer, in a large room on the top floor of an old house on the North Side in Chicago. It was August and the night was hot. Until after midnight I sat – the sweat trickling down my back – under a lamp, labouring to feel my way into the lives of the fanciful people who were trying also to live in the tale on which I was at work.

It was a hopeless affair.

I became involved in the efforts of the shadowy people, and they in turn became involved in the fact of the hot uncomfortable room, in the fact that, although it was what the farmers of the Middle West call 'good corn-growing weather,' it was plain hell to be alive in Chicago. Hand in hand the shadowy people of my fanciful world and myself groped our way through a forest in which the leaves had all been burned off the trees. The hot ground burned the shoes off our feet. We were striving to make our way through the forest and into some cool, beautiful city. The fact is, as you will clearly understand, I was a little off my head.

When I gave up the struggle and got to my feet the chairs in the room danced about. They also were running aimlessly through a burning land and striving to reach some mythical city. 'I'd better get out of here and go for a walk, or go jump into the lake and cool myself off,' I thought.

I went down out of my room and into the street. On a lower floor of the house lived two burlesque actresses, who had just come in from their evening's work and who now sat in their room talking. As I reached the street something heavy whirled past my head and broke on the stone pavement. A white liquid spurted over my clothes and the voice of one of the actresses could be heard coming from the one lighted room of the house. 'Oh, hell! We live such damned lives, we do, and we work in such a town! A dog is better off! And now they are going to take booze away from us too! I come home from working in that hot theatre on a hot night like this, and what do I see – a half-filled bottle of spoiled milk standing on a window-sill!

'I won't stand it! I got to smash everything!' she cried.

I walked eastward from my house. From the north-western end of the city great hordes of men, women and children had come to spend the night out of doors, by the shore of the lake. It was stifling hot there, too, and the air was heavy with a sense of struggle. On a few hundred acres of flat land, that had formerly been a swamp, some two million people were fighting for the peace and quiet of sleep and not getting it. Out of the half-darkness, beyond the little strip of park-land at the water's edge, the huge empty houses of Chicago's fashionable folk made a greyish-blue blot against the sky. 'Thank the gods,' I thought, 'there are some people who can get out of here, who can go to the mountains or the seashore or to Europe.' I stumbled in the half-darkness over the legs of a woman who was lying and trying to sleep on the grass. A baby lay beside her, and when she sat up it began to cry. I muttered an apology and stepped aside, and as I did so my foot struck a half-filled milk bottle and I knocked it over, the milk running out on the grass. 'Oh, I'm sorry. Please forgive me,' I cried. 'Never mind,' the woman answered, 'the milk is sour.'

He is a tall, stoop-shouldered man with prematurely greyed hair, and worked as a copy-writer in an advertising agency in Chicago — an agency where I also have sometimes been employed — and on that night in August I met him, walking with quick, eager strides along the shore of the lake and past the tired, petulant people. He did not see me at first, and I wondered at the evidence of life in him when everyone else seemed half-dead; but a street lamp hanging over a nearby roadway threw its light down upon my face and he pounced. 'Here you, come up to my place,' he cried sharply. 'I've got something to show you. I was on my way down to see you. That's where I was going,' he lied as he hurried me along.

We went to his apartment on a street leading back from the lake and the park. German, Polish, Italian and Jewish families, equipped with soiled blankets and the ever-present half-filled bottles of milk, had come prepared to spend the night out of doors; but the American families in the crowd were giving up the struggle to find a cool spot, and a little stream of them trickled along the sidewalk, going back to hot beds in the hot houses.

It was past one o'clock and my friend's apartment was disorderly as well as hot. He explained that his wife, with their two children, had gone home to visit her mother on a farm near Springfield, Illinois.

We took off our coats and sat down. My friend's thin cheeks were flushed and his eyes shone. 'You know — well — you see,' he began, and then hesitated and laughed like an embarrassed schoolboy. 'Well now,' he began again, 'I've long been wanting to write something real, something besides advertisements. I suppose I'm silly, but that's the way I am. It's been my dream to write something stirring and big. I suppose it's the dream of a lot of advertising writers, eh? Now look here – don't you go laughing. I think I've done it.'

He explained that he had written something concerning Chicago, the capital and heart, as he said, of the whole Central West. He grew angry. 'People come here from the East or from farms, or from little holes of towns like I came from and they think it smart to run Chicago into the ground,' he declared. 'I thought I'd show 'em up,' he added, jumping up and walking nervously about the room.

He handed me many sheets of paper covered with hastily scrawled words, but I protested and asked him to read it aloud. He did, standing with his face turned away from me. There was a quiver in his voice. The thing he had written concerned some mythical town I had never seen. He called it Chicago, but in the same breath spoke of great streets flaming with colour, ghostlike buildings flung up into night skies, and a river running down a path of gold into the boundless West. It was the city, I told myself, I and the people of my story had been trying to find earlier on that same evening, when because of the heat I went a little off my head and could not work any more. The people of the city, he had written about, were a cool-headed, brave people, marching forward to some spiritual triumph, the promise of which was inherent in the physical aspects of the town.

Now I am one who, by the careful cultivation of certain traits in my character, have succeeded in building up the more brutal side of my nature, but I cannot knock women and children down in order to get aboard Chicago street-cars, nor can I tell an author to his face that I think his work is rotten.

'You're all right, Ed. You're great. You've knocked out a regular soc-dolager of a masterpiece here. Why you sound as good as Henry Mencken writing about Chicago as the literary centre of America, and you've lived in Chicago and he never did. The only thing I can see you've missed is a little something about the stockyards, and you can put that in later,' I added, and prepared to depart.

'What's this?' I asked, picking up a half-dozen sheets of paper that lay on the floor by my chair. I read it eagerly. And when I had finished reading it he stammered and apologized and then, stepping across the room, jerked the sheets out of my hand and threw them out at an open window.

'I wish you hadn't seen that. It's something else I wrote about Chicago,' he explained. He was flustered. 'You see the night was so hot, and, down at the office, I had to write a condensed-milk advertisement, just as I was sneaking away to come home and work on this other thing, and the street-car was so crowded and the people stank so, and when I finally got home here – the wife being gone – the place was a mess. Well, I couldn't write and I was sore. It's been my chance, you see, the wife and kids being gone and the house being quiet. I went for a walk. I think I went a little off my head. Then I came home and wrote that stuff I've just thrown out of the window.'

He grew cheerful again. 'Oh, well – it's all right. Writing that fool thing stirred me up and enabled me to write this other stuff, this real stuff I showed you first, about Chicago.'

And so I went home and to bed, having in this odd way stumbled upon another bit of the kind of writing that is –

for better or worse – really presenting the lives of the
people of these towns and cities – sometimes in prose,
sometimes in stirring colourful song. It was the kind of
thing Mr. Sandburg or Mr. Masters might have done
after an evening's walk on a hot night in, say, West Con-
gress Street in Chicago.

The thing I had read of Ed's centred about a half-filled
bottle of spoiled milk standing dim in the moonlight on a
window-sill. There had been a moon earlier on that
August evening, a new moon, a thin crescent golden streak
in the sky. What had happened to my friend, the adver-
tising-writer, was something like this – I figured it all out
as I lay sleepless in bed after our talk.

I am sure I do not know whether or not it is true that
all advertising-writers and newspaper men want to do
other kinds of writing, but Ed did all right. The August
day that had preceded the hot night had been a hard one
for him to get through. All day he had been wanting to be
at home in his quiet apartment producing literature, rather
than sitting in an office and writing advertisements. In the
late afternoon, when he had thought his desk cleared for
the day, the boss of the copy writers came and ordered him
to write a page advertisement for the magazines on the
subject of condensed milk. 'We got a chance to get a
new account if we can knock out some crackerjack stuff
in a hurry,' he said. 'I'm sorry to have to put it up to you
on such a rotten hot day, Ed, but we're up against it.
Let's see if you've got some of the old pep in you. Get
down to hardpan now and knock out something snappy
and unusual before you go home.'

Ed had tried. He put away the thoughts he had been
having about the city beautiful – the glowing city of the

plains – and got right down to business. He thought about milk, milk for little children, the Chicagoans of the future, milk that would produce a little cream to put in the coffee of advertising-writers in the morning, sweet fresh milk to keep all his brother and sister Chicagoans robust and strong. What Ed really wanted was a long cool drink of something with a kick in it, but he tried to make himself think he wanted a drink of milk. He gave himself over to thoughts of milk, milk condensed and yellow, milk warm from the cows his father owned when he was a boy – his mind launched a little boat and he set out on a sea of milk.

Out of it all he got what is called an original advertisement. The sea of milk on which he sailed became a mountain of cans of condensed milk, and out of that fancy he got his idea. He made a crude sketch for a picture showing wide rolling green fields with white farm-houses. Cows grazed on the green hills and at one side of the picture a barefooted boy was driving a herd of Jersey cows out of the sweet fair land and down a lane into a kind of funnel at the small end of which was a tin of the condensed milk. Over the picture he put a heading: 'The health and freshness of a whole countryside is condensed into one can of Whitney-Wells Condensed Milk.' The head copy writer said it was a humdinger.

And then Ed went home. He wanted to begin writing about the city beautiful at once and so didn't go out to dinner, but fished about in the ice-chest and found some cold meat out of which he made himself a sandwich. Also, he poured himself a glass of milk, but it was sour. 'Oh, damn!' he said and poured it into the kitchen sink.

As Ed explained to me later, he sat down and tried to

begin writing his real stuff at once, but he couldn't seem to get into it. The last hour in the office, the trip home in the hot smelly car, and the taste of the sour milk in his mouth had jangled his nerves. The truth is that Ed has a rather sensitive, finely balanced nature, and it had got mussed up.

He took a walk and tried to think, but his mind wouldn't stay where he wanted it to. Ed is now a man of nearly forty and on that night his mind ran back to his young manhood in the city — and stayed there. Like other boys who had become grown men in Chicago, he had come to the city from a farm at the edge of a prairie town, and like all such town and farm boys, he had come filled with vague dreams.

What things he had hungered to do and be in Chicago! What he had done you can fancy. For one thing he had got himself married and now lived in the apartment on the North Side. To give a real picture of his life during the twelve or fifteen years that had slipped away since he was a young man would involve writing a novel, and that is not my purpose.

Anyway, there he was in his room — come home from his walk — and it was hot and quiet and he could not manage to get into his masterpiece. How still it was in the apartment with the wife and children away! His mind stayed on the subject of his youth in the city.

He remembered a night of his young manhood when he had gone out to walk, just as he did on that August evening. Then his life wasn't complicated by the fact of the wife and children and he lived alone in his room; but something had got on his nerves then, too. On that evening long ago he grew restless in his room and went out to walk. It was summer and first he went down by the river where ships were being loaded and then to a crowded park where girls and young fellows walked about.

He grew bold and spoke to a woman who sat alone on a park bench. She let him sit beside her and, because it was dark and she was silent, he began to talk. The night had made him sentimental. 'Human beings are such hard things to get at. I wish I could get close to someone,' he said. 'Oh, you go on! What you doing? You ain't trying to kid someone?' asked the woman.

Ed jumped up and walked away. He went into a long street lined with dark silent buildings and then stopped and looked about. What he wanted was to believe that in the apartment buildings were people who lived intense eager lives, who had great dreams, who were capable of great adventures. 'They are really only separated from me by the brick walls,' was what he told himself on that night.

It was then that the milk bottle theme first got hold of him. He went into an alleyway to look at the backs of the apartment buildings and, on that evening also, there was a moon. Its light fell upon a long row of half-filled bottles standing on window-sills.

Something within him went a little sick and he hurried out of the alleyway and into the street. A man and woman walked past him and stopped before the entrance to one of the buildings. Hoping they might be lovers, he concealed himself in the entrance to another building to listen to their conversation.

The couple turned out to be a man and wife and they were quarrelling. Ed heard the woman's voice saying: 'You come in here. You can't put that over on me. You say you just want to take a walk, but I know you.

You want to go out and blow in some money. What I'd like to know is why you don't loosen up a little for me.'

That is the story of what happened to Ed, when, as a young man, he went to walk in the city in the evening, and when he had become a man of forty and went out of his house wanting to dream and to think of a city beautiful, much the same sort of thing happened again. Perhaps the writing of the condensed-milk advertisement and the taste of the sour milk he had got out of the ice-box had something to do with his mood; but, anyway, milk bottles, like a refrain in a song, got into his brain. They seemed to sit and mock at him from the windows of all the buildings in all the streets, and when he turned to look at people, he met the crowds from the West and the North-west Sides going to the park and the lake. At the head of each little group of people marched a woman who carried a milk bottle in her hand.

And so, on that August night, Ed went home angry and disturbed, and in anger wrote of his city. Like the burlesque actress in my own house he wanted to smash something, and, as milk bottles were in his mind, he wanted to smash milk bottles. 'I could grasp the neck of a milk bottle. It fits the hand so neatly. I could kill a man or woman with such a thing,' he thought desperately.

He wrote, you see, the five or six sheets I had read in that mood and then felt better. And after that he wrote about the ghostlike buildings flung into the sky by the hands of a brave adventurous people and about the river that runs down a path of gold, and into the boundless West.

As you have already concluded, the city he described in his masterpiece was lifeless, but the city he, in a queer way, expressed in what he wrote about the milk bottle could not be forgotten. It frightened you a little, but there it was, and in spite of his anger, or perhaps because of it, a lovely singing quality had got into the thing. In those few scrawled pages the miracle had been worked. I was a fool not to have put the sheets into my pocket. When I went down out of his apartment that evening I did look for them in a dark alleyway, but they had become lost in a sea of rubbish that had leaked over the tops of a long row of tin ash-cans that stood at the foot of a stairway leading from the back doors of the apartments above.

*

It had been a disastrous year in Will's family. The Appletons lived on one of the outlying streets of Bidwell, and Will's father was a house painter. In early February, when there was deep snow on the ground, and a cold bitter wind blew about the houses, Will's mother suddenly died. He was seventeen years old then, and rather a big fellow for his age.

The mother's death happened abruptly, without warning, as a sleepy man kills a fly with the hand in a warm room on a summer day. On one February day there she was coming in at the kitchen door of the Appletons' house, from hanging the wash out on the line in the back yard, and warming her long hands, covered with blue veins, by holding them over the kitchen stove – and then looking about at the children with that half-hidden, shy smile of hers – there she was like that, as the three children had always known her, and then, but a week later, she was cold in death and lying in her coffin in the place vaguely spoken of in the family as 'the other room.'

After that, and when summer came and the family was trying hard to adjust itself to the new conditions, there came another disaster. Up to the very moment when it happened it looked as though Tom Appleton, the house painter, was in for a prosperous season. The two boys, Fred and Will, were to be his assistants that year.

To be sure Fred was only fifteen, but he was one to lend a quick alert hand at almost any undertaking. For example, when there was a job of paper-hanging to be done, he was the fellow to spread on the paste, helped by an occasional sharp word from his father.

Down off his step-ladder Tom Appleton hopped and ran to the long board where the paper was spread out. He liked this business of having two assistants about. Well, you see, one had the feeling of being at the head of something, of managing affairs. He grabbed the paste-brush out of Fred's hand. 'Don't spare the paste,' he shouted. 'Slap her on like this. Spread her out – so. Do be sure to catch all the edges.'

It was all very warm, and comfortable, and nice, working at paper-hanging jobs in the houses on the March and April days. When it was cold or rainy outside, stoves were set up in the new houses being built, and in houses already inhabited the folks moved out of the rooms to be papered, spread newspapers on the floors over the carpets and put sheets over the furniture left in the rooms. Outside it rained or snowed, but inside it was warm and cosy.

To the Appletons it seemed, at the time, as though the death of the mother had drawn them closer together. Both Will and Fred felt it, perhaps Will the more consciously. The family was rather in the hole financially – the mother's funeral had cost a good deal of money, and Fred was being allowed to stay out of school. That pleased him. When they worked in a house where there were other children, they came home from school in the late afternoon and looked in through the door to where Fred was spreading paste over the sheets of wall-paper. He made a slapping sound with the brush, but did not look at them. 'Ah, go on, you kids,' he thought. This was a man's business he was up to. Will and his father were on the step-ladders, putting the sheets carefully into place on the ceilings and walls. 'Does she match down there?' the father asked sharply. 'Oh-kay, go ahead,' Will replied. When the sheet was in place Fred ran and rolled out the laps with a little wooden roller. How jealous the kids of the house were. It would be a long time before any of them could stay out of school and do a man's work, as Fred was doing.

And then in the evening, walking homeward, it was nice, too. Will and Fred had been provided with suits of white overalls that were now covered with dried paste and spots of paint and looked really professional. They kept them on and drew their overcoats on over them. Their hands were stiff with paste, too. On Main Street the lights. were lighted, and other men passing called to Tom Appleton. He was called Tony in the town. 'Hello, Tony!' some storekeeper shouted. It was rather too bad, Will thought, that his father hadn't more dignity. He was too boyish. Young boys growing up and merging into manhood do not fancy fathers being too boyish. Tom Appleton played a cornet in the Bidwell Silver Cornet Band and didn't do the job very well – rather made a mess of it, when there was a bit of solo work to be done – but was so well liked by the other members of the band that no one said anything. And then he talked so grandly about music, and about the lip of a cornet player, that everyone thought he must be all right. 'He has an education. I tell you what, Tony Appleton knows a lot. He's a smart one,' the other members of the band were always saying to each other.

'Well, the devil! A man should grow up after a time, perhaps. When a man's wife had died but such a short time before, it was just as well to walk through Main Street with more dignity – for the time being, anyway.'

Tom Appleton had a way of winking at men he passed in the street, as though to say, 'Well, now I've got my kids with me, and we won't say anything, but didn't you and I

132

have the very hell of a time last Wednesday night, eh? Mum's the word, old pal. Keep everything quiet. There are gay times ahead for you and me. We'll cut loose, you bet, when you and me are out together next time.'

Will grew a little angry about something he couldn't exactly understand. His father stopped in front of Jake Mann's meat market. 'You kids go along home. Tell Kate I am bringing a steak. I'll be right on your heels,' he said.

He would get the steak and then he would go into Alf Geiger's saloon and get a good, stiff drink of whisky. There would be no one now to bother about smelling it on his breath when he got home later. Not that his wife had ever said anything when he wanted a drink – but you know how a man feels when there's a woman in the house. 'Why – hello, Bildad Smith – how's the old game leg? Come on, have a little nip with me. Were you on Main Street last band meeting night and did you hear us do that new gallop? It's a humdinger. Turkey White did that trombone solo simply grand.'

Will and Fred had got beyond Main Street now, and Will took a small pipe with a curved stem out of his overcoat pocket and lighted it. 'I'll bet I could hang a ceiling without father there at all, if only someone would give me a chance,' he said. Now that his father was no longer present to embarrass him with his lack of dignity, he felt comfortable and happy. Also, it was something to be able to smoke a pipe without discomfiture. When mother was alive she was always kissing a fellow when he came home at night, and then one had to be mighty careful about smoking. Now it was different. One had become a man and one accepted manhood with its responsibilities. 'Don't it make you sick at all?' Fred asked. 'Huh, naw!' Will answered contemptuously.

The new disaster to the family came late in August, just when the fall work was all ahead, and the prospects good, too. A. P. Wrigley, the jeweller, had just built a big, new house and barn on a farm he had bought the year before. It was a mile out of town on the Turner pike.

That would be a job to set the Appletons up for the winter. The house was to have three coats outside, with all the work inside, and the barn was to have two coats – and the two boys were to work with their father and were to have regular wages.

And just to think of the work to be done inside that house made Tom Appleton's mouth water. He talked of it all the time, and in the evenings liked to sit in a chair in the Appletons' front yard, get some neighbour over, and then go on about it. How he slung house-painter's lingo about! The doors and cupboards were to be grained in imitation of weathered oak, the front door was to be curly maple, and there was to be black walnut, too. Well, there wasn't another painter in the town could imitate all the various kinds of wood as Tom could. Just show him the wood, or tell him – you didn't have to show him anything. Name what you wanted – that was enough. To be sure a man had to have the right tools, but give him the tools and then just go off and leave everything to him. What the devil! When A. P. Wrigley gave him this new house to do, he showed he was a man who knew what he was doing.

As for the practical side of the matter, everyone in the family knew that the Wrigley job meant a safe winter. There wasn't any speculation, as when taking work on the contract plan. All work was to be paid for by the day, and the boys were to have their wages, too. It meant new suits for the boys, a new dress and maybe a hat for Kate, the house rent paid all winter, potatoes in the cellar. It meant safety – that was the truth.

In the evenings, sometimes, Tom got out his tools and looked at them. Brushes and graining-tools were spread out on the kitchen table, and Kate and the boys gathered about. It was Fred's job to see that all brushes were kept clean and, one by one, Tom ran his fingers over them, and then worked them back and forth over the palm of his hand. 'This is a camel's hair,' he said, picking a soft fine-haired brush up and handing it to Will. 'I paid four dollars and eighty cents for that.' Will also worked it back and forth over the palm of his hand, just as his father had done, and then Kate picked it up and did the same thing. 'It's as soft as the cat's back,' she said. Will thought that rather silly. He looked forward to the day when he would have brushes, ladders and pots of his own, and could show them off before people, and through his mind went words he had picked up from his father's talk. One spoke of the 'heel' and 'toe' of a brush. The way to put on varnish was to 'flow' it on. Will knew all the words of his trade now and didn't have to talk like one of the kind of muts who just does, now and then, a jack job of house painting.

On the fatal evening a surprise party was held for Mr. and Mrs. Bardshare, who lived just across the road from the Appletons on Piety Hill. That was a chance for Tom Appleton. In any such affair he liked to have a hand in the arrangements. 'Come on now, we'll make her go with a bang. They'll be sitting in the house after supper, and Bill Bardshare will be in his stocking feet, and Ma Bard-share washing the dishes. They won't be expecting nothing, and we'll slip up, all dressed in our Sunday clothes, and let out a whoop. I'll bring my cornet and let out a blast on that too. 'What in Sam Hill is that?' Say, I can just see Bill Bardshare jumping up and beginning to swear, thinking we're a gang of kids come to bother him, like Hallowe'en, or something like that. You just get the grub, and I'll make the coffee over to my house and bring it over hot. I'll get ahold of two big pots and make a whooping lot of it.'

In the Appleton house all was in a flurry. Tom, Will and Fred were painting a barn, three miles out of town, but they knocked off work at four and Tom got the farmer's son to drive them to town. He himself had to wash up, take a bath in a tub in the wood-shed, shave and everything — just like Sunday. He looked more like a boy than a man when he got all dogged up.

And then the family had to have supper over and done with a little after six, and Tom didn't dare go outside the house until dark. It wouldn't do to have the Bardshares see him so fixed up. It was their wedding anniversary, and they might suspect something. He kept trotting about the house, and occasionally looked out of the front window toward the Bardshare house. 'You kid, you,' Kate said, laughing. Sometimes she talked up to him like that, and after she said it he went upstairs, and getting out his cornet blew on it, so softly you could hardly hear him downstairs. When he did that you couldn't tell how badly he played, as when the band was going it on Main Street and he had to carry a passage right through alone. He sat in the room upstairs, thinking. When Kate laughed at him it was like having his wife back, alive. There was the same shy, sarcastic gleam in her eyes.

Well, it was the first time he had been out anywhere since his wife had died, and there might be some people think it would be better if he stayed at home now — look better, that is. When he had shaved he had cut his chin, and the blood had come. After a time he went downstairs and stood before the looking-glass hung above the kitchen sink, and dabbed at the spot with the wet end of a towel.

Will and Fred stood about.

Will's mind was working — perhaps Kate's, too. 'Was there — could it be? — well, at such a party — only older people invited — there were always two or three widow women thrown in for good measure, as it were.'

Kate didn't want any woman fooling around her kitchen. She was twenty years old.

'And it was just as well not to have any monkey-shine talk about motherless children,' such as Tom might indulge in. Even Fred thought that. There was a little wave of resentment against Tom in the house. It was a wave that didn't make much noise, just crept, as it were, softly, up a low sandy beach.

'Widow women went to such places, and then, of course, people were always going home in couples.' Both Kate and Will had the same picture in mind. It was late at night, and in fancy they were both peeking out at front upper windows of the Appleton house. There were all the people coming out at the front door of the Bardshare house, and Bill Bardshare was standing there and holding the door open. He had managed to sneak away during the evening, and got his Sunday clothes on all right.

And the couples were coming out. 'There was that woman now, that widow, Mrs. Childers.' She had been married twice, both husbands dead now, and she lived away over Maumee Pike way. 'What makes a woman of her age want to act silly like that? It is the very devil how a woman can keep looking young and handsome after she has buried two men. There are some who say that, even when her last husband was alive –'

'But whether that's true or not, what makes her want to act and talk silly that way?' Now her face is turned to the light and she is saying to old Bill Bardshare, 'Sleep light, sleep tight, sweet dreams to you to-night.'

'It's only what one may expect when one's father lacks a sense of dignity. There is that old fool Tom now, hopping out of the Bardshare house like a kid, and running right up to Mrs. Childers. "May I see you home?" he is saying, while all the others are laughing and smiling knowingly. It makes one's blood run cold to see such a thing.'

'Well, fill up the pots. Let's get the old coffee-pots started, Kate. The gang'll be creeping along up the street pretty soon now,' Tom shouted self-consciously, skipping busily about and breaking the little circle of thoughts in the house.

What happened was that – just as darkness came, and when all the people were in the front yard before the Appleton house – Tom went and got it into his head to try to carry his cornet and two big coffee-pots at the same time. Why didn't he leave the coffee until later? There the people were in the dusk outside the house, and there was that kind of low whispering and tittering that always goes on at such a time – and then Tom stuck his head out at the door and shouted, 'Let her go!'

And then he must have gone quite crazy, for he ran back into the kitchen and grabbed both of the big coffee-

pots, hanging on to his cornet at the same time. Of course
he stumbled in the darkness in the road outside and fell, and
of course all of that boiling hot coffee had to spill right over
him.

It was terrible. The flood of boiling hot coffee made
steam under his thick clothes, and there he lay screaming
with the pain of it. What a confusion! He just writhed
and screamed, and the people ran 'round and 'round in the
half-darkness like crazy things. Was it some kind of joke
the crazy fellow was up to at the last minute? Tom always
was such a devil to think up things. 'You should see
him down at Alf Geigers, sometimes on Saturday nights,
imitating the way Joe Douglas got out on a limb, and then
sawed it off between himself and the tree, and the look
on Joe's face when the limb began to crack. It would
make you laugh until you screamed to see him imitate
that.'

'But what now? My God!' There was Kate Appleton
trying to tear her father's clothes off, and crying and whim-
pering, and young Will Appleton knocking people aside.
'Say, the man's hurt! What's happened? My God! Run
for the doctor, someone. He's burnt, something awful!'

Early in October Will Appleton sat in the smoking-car
of a day train that runs between Cleveland and Buffalo.
His destination was Erie, Pennsylvania, and he had got on
the passenger train at Ashtabula, Ohio. Just why his destination was Erie he couldn't very easily have explained.
He was going there anyway, going to get a job in a factory
or on the docks there. Perhaps it was just a quirk of the
mind that had made him decide upon Erie. It wasn't as big
as Cleveland, or Buffalo, or Toledo, or Chicago, or any one

of a lot of other cities to which he might have gone, looking for work.

At Ashtabula he came into the car and slid into a seat beside a little old man. His own clothes were wet and wrinkled, and his hair, eyebrows and ears were black with coal dust.

At the moment, there was in him a kind of bitter dislike of his native town, Bidwell. 'Sakes alive, a man couldn't get any work there – not in the winter.' After the accident to his father, and the spoiling of all the family plans, he had managed to find employment during September on the farms. He worked for a time with a threshing crew, and then got work cutting corn. It was all right. 'A man made a dollar a day and board, and as he wore overalls all the time, he didn't wear out no clothes. Still and all, the time when a fellow could make any money in Bidwell was past now, and the burns on his father's body had gone pretty deep, and he might be laid up for months.'

Will had just made up his mind one day, after he had tramped about all morning from farm to farm without finding work, and then he had gone home and told Kate. 'Dang it all,' he hadn't intended lighting out right away – had thought he would stay about for a week or two, maybe. Well, he would go up town in the evening, dressed up in his best clothes, and stand around. 'Hello, Harry, what you going to do this winter? I thought I would run over to Erie, Pennsylvania. I got an offer in a factory over there. Well, so long – if I don't see you again.'

Kate hadn't seemed to understand, had seemed in an almighty hurry about getting him off. It was a shame she couldn't have a little more heart. Still, Kate was all right – worried a good deal, no doubt. After their talk she had just said, 'Yes, I think that's best, you had better go,' and had gone to change the bandages on Tom's legs and back. The father was sitting among pillows in a rocking-chair in the front room.

Will went upstairs and put his things, overalls and a few shirts, into a bundle. Then he went downstairs and took a walk – went out along a road that led into the country, and stopped on a bridge. It was near a place where he and other kids used to come swimming on summer afternoons. A thought had come into his head. There was a young fellow worked in Pawsey's jewellery store came to see Kate sometimes on Sunday evenings, and they went off to walk together. 'Did Kate want to get married?' If she did, his going away now might be for good. He hadn't thought about that before. On that afternoon, and quite suddenly, all the world outside of Bidwell seemed huge and terrible to him and a few secret tears came into his eyes, but he managed to choke them back. For just a moment his mouth opened and closed queerly, like the mouth of a fish when you take it out of the water and hold it in your hand.

When he returned to the house at supper-time things were better. He had left his bundle on a chair in the kitchen and Kate had wrapped it more carefully, and had put in a number of things he had forgotten. His father called him into the front room. 'It's all right, Will. Every young fellow ought to take a whirl out in the world. I did it myself, at about your age,' Tom had said, a little pompously.

Then supper was served, and there was apple-pie. That was a luxury the Appletons had perhaps better not have indulged in at that time, but Will knew Kate had baked it during the afternoon – it might be as a way of showing him how she felt. Eating two large slices had rather set him up.

And then, before he realized how the time was slipping away, ten o'clock had come, and it was time for him to go. He was going to beat his way out of town on a freight train, and there was a local going toward Cleveland at ten o'clock. Fred had gone off to bed, and his father was asleep in the rocking-chair in the front room. He had picked up his bundle, and Kate had put on her hat. 'I'm going to see you off,' she had said.

Will and Kate had walked in silence along the streets to where he was to wait, in the shadow of Whaley's Warehouse, until the freight came along. Later, when he thought back over that evening, he was glad that, although she was three years older, he was taller than Kate.

How vividly everything that happened later stayed in his mind. After the train came, and he had crawled into an empty coal car, he sat hunched up in a corner. Overhead he could see the sky, and when the train stopped at towns there was always the chance the car in which he was concealed would be shoved into a siding, and left. The brakemen walked along the tracks beside the car shouting to each other, and their lanterns made little splashes of light in the darkness.

'How black the sky!' After a time it began to rain. 'His suit would be in a pretty mess. After all, a fellow couldn't come right out and ask his sister if she intended to marry. If Kate married, then his father would also marry again. It was all right for a young woman like Kate, but for a man of forty to think of marriage – the devil! Why didn't Tom Appleton have more dignity? After all, Fred was only a kid, and a new woman coming in, to be his mother – that might be all right for a kid.'

All during that night on the freight train Will had thought a good deal about marriage — rather vague thoughts — coming and going like birds flying in and out of a bush. It was all a matter — this business of man and woman — that did not touch him very closely — not yet. The matter of having a home — that was something else. A home was something at a fellow's back. When one went off to work all week at some farm, and at night maybe went into a strange room to sleep, there was always the Appleton house — floating, as it were, like a picture at the back of the mind — the Appleton house, and Kate moving about. She had been up town, and now had come home and was going up the stairs. Tom Appleton was fussing about in the kitchen. He liked a bite before he went off to bed for the night, but presently he would go upstairs and into his own room. He liked to smoke his pipe before he slept, and sometimes he got out his cornet and blew two or three soft sad notes.

At Cleveland Will had crawled off of the freight train and had gone across the city in a street car. Working-men were just going to the factories and he passed among them unnoticed. If his clothes were crumpled and soiled, their clothes weren't so fine. The working-men were all silent, looking at the car floor, or out at the car windows. Long rows of factories stood along the streets through which the car moved.

He had been lucky, and had caught another freight out of a place called Collinswood at eight, but at Ashtabul had made up his mind it would be better to drop off the freight and take a passenger train. If he was to live in Erie, it would be just as well to arrive looking more like a gentleman and having paid his fare.

As he sat in the smoking-car of the train he did not feel much like a gentleman. The coal dust had got into his hair and the rain had washed it in long dirty streaks down over his face. His clothes were badly soiled and wanted cleaning and brushing, and the paper package in which his overalls and shirts were tied had become torn and dirty.

Outside the train window the sky was grey, and no doubt the night was going to turn cold. Perhaps there would be a cold rain.

It was an odd thing about the towns through which the train kept passing – all of the houses in all the towns looked cold and forbidding. 'Dang it all.' In Bidwell, before the night when his father got so badly burned, being such a fool about old Bill Bardshare's party, all the houses had always seemed warm, cosy places. When one was alone, one walked along the streets whistling. At night warm lights shone through the windows of the houses. 'John Wyatt, the drayman, lives in that house. His wife has a wen on her neck. In that barn over there old Doctor Musgrave keeps his bony old white horse. The horse looks like the devil, but you bet he can go.'

Will squirmed about on the car seat. The old man who sat beside him was small, almost as small as Fred, and he wore a queer-looking suit. The pants were brown, and the coat checked, grey and black. There was a small leather case on the floor at his feet.

Long before the man spoke Will knew what would happen. It was bound to turn out that such a fellow played a cornet. He was a man old in years, but there was no dignity in him. Will remembered his father's marchings through the main street of Bidwell with the band. It was some great day, Fourth of July, perhaps, and all the people were assembled, and there was Tony Appleton, making a show of blowing his cornet at a great rate. Did all the people along the street know how badly he played, and was there a kind of conspiracy that kept grown men from laughing at each other? In spite of the seriousness of his own situation a smile crept over Will's face.

The little man at his side smiled in return.

'Well,' he began, not stopping for anything, but plunging headlong into a tale concerning some dissatisfaction he felt with life, 'well, you see before you a man who is up against it, young fellow.' The old man tried to laugh at his own words, but did not make much of a success of it. His lip trembled. 'I got to go home like a dog, with my tail 'twixt my legs,' he declared abruptly.

The old man balanced back and forth between two impulses. He had met a young man on a train, and hungered for companionship, and one got oneself in with others by being jolly, a little gay, perhaps. When one met a stranger on a train one told a story – 'By the way, Mister, I heard a new one the other day – perhaps you haven't heard it? It's about the miner up in Alaska who hadn't seen a woman for years.' One began in that way, and then later, perhaps, spoke of oneself, and one's affairs.

But the old man wanted to plunge at once into his own story. He talked, saying sad discouraged words, while his eyes kept smiling with a peculiar appealing little smile. 'If the words uttered by my lips annoy or bore you, do not pay any attention to them. I am really a jolly fellow although I am an old man, and not of much use any more,' the eyes were saying. The eyes were pale blue and watery. How strange to see them set in the head of an old man. They belonged in the head of a lost dog. The smile was not really a smile. 'Don't kick me, young fellow. If you can't give me anything to eat, scratch my head. At least show you are a fellow of good intentions. I've been kicked about quite enough.' It was so very evident the eyes were speaking a language of their own.

Will found himself smiling sympathetically. It was true there was something dog-like in the little old man, and Will was pleased with himself for having so quickly caught the sense of him. 'One who can see things with his eyes will perhaps get along all right in the world, after all,' he thought. His thoughts wandered away from the old man. In Bidwell there was an old woman lived alone and owned a shepherd dog. Every summer she decided to cut away the dog's coat, and then – at the last moment and after she had in fact started the job – she changed her mind. Well, she grasped a long pair of scissors firmly in her hand and started on the dog's flanks. Her hand trembled a little. 'Shall I go ahead, or shall I stop?' After two minutes she gave up the job. 'It makes him look too ugly,' she thought, justifying her timidity.

Later the hot days came, the dog went about with his tongue hanging out, and again the old woman took the scissors in her hand. The dog stood patiently waiting, but, when she had cut a long wide furrow through the thick hair of his back, she stopped again. In a sense, and to her way of looking at the matter, cutting away his splendid coat was like cutting away a part of himself. She couldn't go on. 'Now there – that made him look worse than ever,' she declared to herself. With a determined air she put the scissors away, and all summer the dog went about looking a little puzzled and ashamed.

Will kept smiling and thinking of the old woman's dog, and then looked again at his companion of the train. The variegated suit the old man wore gave him something of the air of the half-sheared shepherd dog. Both had the same puzzled, ashamed air.

Now Will had begun using the old man for his own ends. There was something inside himself that wanted facing he didn't want to face – not yet. Ever since he had left home, in fact ever since that day when he had come home from the country and had told Kate of his intention to set out into the world, he had been dodging something. If one thought of the little old man, and of the half-sheared dog, one did not have to think of oneself.

One thought of Bidwell on a summer afternoon. There was the old woman who owned the dog, standing on the porch of her house, and the dog had run down to the gate. In the winter, when his coat had again fully grown, the dog would bark and make a great fuss about a boy passing in the street, but now he started to bark and growl, and then stopped. 'I look like the devil, and I'm attracting unnecessary attention to myself,' the dog seemed to have decided suddenly. He ran furiously down to the gate, opened his mouth to bark, and then, quite abruptly, changed his mind and trotted back to the house with his tail between his legs.

Will kept smiling at his own thoughts. For the first time since he had left Bidwell he felt quite cheerful.

And now the old man was telling a story of himself and his life, but Will wasn't listening. Within the young man a cross-current of impulses had been set up, and he was like one standing silently in the hallway of a house and listening to two voices, talking at a distance. The voices came from two widely separated rooms of the house and one couldn't make up one's mind to which voice to listen.

To be sure, the old man was another cornet player like his father – he was a horn-blower. That was his horn in the little worn leather case on the car floor.

And after he had reached middle age, and after his first wife had died, he had married again. He had a little property then and, in a foolish moment, went and made it all over to his second wife, who was fifteen years younger than himself. She took the money and bought a large house in the factory district of Erie, and then began taking in boarders.

There was the old man, feeling lost, of no account in his own house. It just came about. One had to think of the boarders – their wants had to be satisfied. His wife had two sons, almost fully grown now, both of whom worked in a factory.

Well, it was all right – everything on the square – the sons paid board all right. Their wants had to be thought of, too. He liked blowing his cornet a while in the evenings, before he went to bed, but it might disturb the others in the house. One got rather desperate going about saying nothing, keeping out of the way, and he had tried getting work in a factory himself, but they wouldn't have him. His grey hairs stood in his way, and so one night he had just got out, had gone to Cleveland, where he had hoped to get a job in a band, in a movie theatre, perhaps. Anyway, it hadn't turned out and now he was going back to Erie and to his wife. He had written and she had told him to come on home.

'They didn't turn me down back there in Cleveland because I'm old. It's because my lip is no good any more,' he explained. His shrunken old lip trembled a little.

Will kept thinking of the old woman's dog. In spite of himself, and when the old man's lip trembled, his lip also trembled.

What was the matter with him?

He stood in the hallway of a house hearing two voices. Was he trying to close his ears to one of them? Did the second voice, the one he had been trying all day, and all the night before, not to hear, did that have something to do with the end of his life in the Appleton house at Bidwell? Was the voice trying to taunt him, trying to tell him that now he was a thing swinging in air, that there was no place to put down his feet? Was he afraid? Of what was he afraid? He had wanted so much to be a man, to stand on his own feet, and now what was the matter with him? Was he afraid of manhood?

He was fighting deperately now. There were tears in the old man's eyes, and Will also began crying silently, and that was the one thing he felt he must not do.

The old man talked on and on, telling the tale of his troubles, but Will could not hear his words. The struggle within was becoming more and more definite. His mind clung to the life of his boyhood, to the life in the Appleton house in Bidwell.

There was Fred, standing in the field of his fancy now, with just the triumphant look in his eyes that came when other boys saw him doing a man's work. A whole series of pictures floated up before Will's mind. He and his father and Fred were painting a barn, and two farmer boys had come along a road and stood looking at Fred, who was on a ladder, putting on paint. They shouted, but Fred wouldn't answer. There was a certain air Fred had – he slapped on the paint, and then, turning his head, spat on the ground.

Tom Appleton's eyes looked into Will's, and there was a smile playing about the corners of the father's eyes and the son's eyes, too. The father and his oldest son were like two men, two workmen, having a delicious little secret between them. They were both looking lovingly at Fred. 'Bless him! He thinks he's a man already.'

And now Tom Appleton was standing in the kitchen of his house, and his brushes were laid out on the kitchen table. Kate was rubbing a brush back and forth over the palm of her hand. 'It's as soft as the cat's back,' she was saying.

Something gripped at Will's throat. As in a dream, he saw his sister Kate walking off along the street on Sunday evening with that young fellow who clerked in the jewellery store. They were going to church. Her being with him meant – well, it perhaps meant the beginning of a new home – it meant the end of the Appleton home.

Will started to climb out of the seat beside the old man in the smoking-car of the train. It had grown almost dark in the car. The old man was still talking, telling his tale over and over. 'I might as well not have any home at all,' he was saying. Was Will about to begin crying aloud on a train, in a strange place, before many strange men? He tried to speak, to make some commonplace remark, but his mouth only opened and closed like the mouth of a fish taken out of the water.

And now the train had run into a train shed, and it was quite dark. Will's hand clutched convulsively into the darkness and alighted upon the old man's shoulder.

Then suddenly the train had stopped, and the two stood half-embracing each other. The tears were quite evident in Will's eyes when a brakeman lighted the overhead lamps in the car, but the luckiest thing in the world had happened. The old man, who had seen Will's tears, thought they were tears of sympathy for his own unfortunate position in life and a look of gratitude came into his blue, watery eyes. Well, this was something new in life for him, too. In one of the pauses, when he had first begun telling his tale, Will had said he was going to Erie to try to get work in some factory, and now, as they got off the train, the old man clung to Will's arm. 'You might as well come live at our house,' he said. A look of hope flared up in the old man's eyes. If he could bring home with him, to his young wife, a new boarder, the gloom of his own home-coming would be somewhat lightened. 'You come on. That's the best thing to do. You just come on with me to our house,' he pleaded, clinging to Will.

Two weeks had passed and Will had, outwardly, and to the eyes of the people about him, settled into his new life as a factory hand at Erie, Pennsylvania.

Then suddenly, on a Saturday evening, the thing happened that he had unconsciously been expecting and dreading ever since the moment when he climbed aboard the freight train in the shadow of Whaley's Warehouse at Bidwell. A letter, containing great news, had come from Kate.

At the moment of their parting, and before he settled himself down out of sight in a corner of the empty coal car on that night of his leaving, he had leaned out for a last look at his sister. She had been standing silently in the shadows of the warehouse, but, just as the train was about to start, stepped toward him, and a light from a distant street lamp fell on her face.

Well, the face did not jump toward Will, but remained dimly outlined in the uncertain light.

Did her lips open and close, as though in an effort to say something to him, or was that an effect produced by the distant, uncertain and wavering light? In the families of working people the dramatic and vital moments of life are passed over in silence. Even in the moments of death and birth, little is said. A child is born to a labourer's wife and he goes into the room. She is in bed, with the little red bundle of new life beside her, and her husband stands a moment, fumblingly, beside the bed. Neither he nor his wife can look directly into each other's eyes. 'Take care of yourself, Ma. Have a good rest,' he says, and hurries out of the room.

In the darkness by the warehouse at Bidwell Kate had taken two or three steps toward Will, and then had stopped. There was a little strip of grass between the warehouse and the tracks, and she stood upon it. Was there a more final farewell trembling on her lips at the moment? A kind of dread had swept over Will, and no doubt Kate had felt the same thing. At the moment she had become altogether the mother in the presence of her child, and the thing within that wanted utterance became submerged. There was a word to be said that she could not say. Her form seemed to sway a little in the darkness and, to Will's eyes, she became a slender indistinct thing. 'Good-bye,' he had whispered into the darkness, and perhaps her lips had formed the same words. Outwardly there had been only the silence, and in the silence she had stood as the train rumbled away.

And now, on the Saturday evening, Will had come home from the factory and had found Kate saying in the letter what she had been unable to say on the night of his departure. The factory closed at five on Saturday and he came home in his overalls and went to his room. He had found the letter on a little broken table under a spluttering oil lamp, by the front door, and had climbed the stairs carrying it in his hand. He read the letter anxiously, waiting as for a hand to come out of the blank wall of the room and strike.

His father was getting better. The deep burns that had taken such a long time to heal were really healing now, and the doctor had said the danger of infection had passed. Kate had found a new and soothing remedy. One took slippery elm and let it lie in milk until it became soft. This applied to the burns enabled Tom to sleep better at night.

As for Fred, Kate and her father had decided he might as well go back to school. It was really too bad for a young boy to miss the chance to get an education, and anyway, there was no work to be had. Perhaps he could get a job, helping in some store on Saturday afternoons.

A woman from the Woman's Relief Corps had had the nerve to come to the Appleton house and ask Kate if the family needed help. Well, Kate had managed to hold herself back, and had been polite, but, had the woman known what was in her mind, her ears would have been itching for a month. The idea!

It had been fine of Will to send a postcard, as soon as he had got to Erie and got a job. As for his sending money home – of course the family would be glad to have anything he could spare – but he wasn't to go depriving himself. 'We've got good credit at the stores. We'll get along all right,' Kate had said stoutly.

And then it was she had added the line, had said the thing she could not say that night when he was leaving.

It concerned herself and her future plans. 'That night when you were going away I wanted to tell you something, but I thought it was silly, talking too soon.' After all, though, Will might as well know she was planning to be married in the spring. What she wanted was for Fred to come and live with her and her husband. He could keep on going to school, and perhaps they could manage so that he could go to college. Someone in the family ought to have a decent education. Now that Will had made his start in life, there was no point in waiting longer before making her own.

Will sat in his tiny room at the top of the huge frame house, owned now by the wife of the old cornet player of the train, and held the letter in his hand. The room was on the third floor, under the roof, in a wing of the house, and beside it was another small room, occupied by the old man himself. Will had taken the room because it was to be had at a low price, and he could manage the room and his meals, get his washing done, send three dollars a week to Kate, and still have left a dollar a week to spend. One could get a little tobacco, and now and then see a movie.

'Ugh!' Will's lips made a little grunting noise as he read Kate's words. He was sitting in a chair, in his oily overalls, and where his fingers gripped the white sheets of the letter there was a little oily smudge. Also his hand trembled a little. He got up, poured water out of a pitcher into a white bowl, and began washing his face and hands.

When he had partly dressed, a visitor came. There was the shuffling sound of weary feet along a hallway, and the cornet player put his head timidly in at the door. The dog-like appealing look Will had noted on the train was still in his eyes. Now he was planning something, a kind of gentle revolt against his wife's power in the house, and he wanted Will's moral support.

For a week he had been coming for talk to Will's room almost every evening. There were two things he wanted. In the evening sometimes, as he sat in his room, he wanted to blow upon his cornet, and he wanted a little money to jingle in his pockets.

And there was a sense in which Will, the new-comer in the house, was his property, did not belong to his wife. Often in the evenings he had talked to the weary and sleepy young workman, until Will's eyes had closed and he snored gently. The old man sat on the one chair in the room, and Will sat on the edge of the bed, while old lips told the tale of a lost youth, boasted a little. When Will's body had slumped down upon the bed the old man got to his feet and moved with cat-like steps about the room. One mustn't raise the voice too loudly, after all. Had Will gone to sleep? The cornet player threw his shoulders back and bold words came, in a half-whisper, from his lips. To tell the truth, he had been a fool about the money he had made over to his wife and, if his wife had taken advantage of him, it wasn't her fault. For his present position in life he had no one to blame but himself. What from the very beginning he had most lacked was boldness. It was a man's duty to be a man and, for a long time, he had been thinking – well, the boarding-house no doubt made a profit and he should have his share. His wife was a good girl all right, but when one came right down to it, all women seemed to lack a sense of a man's position in life.

'I'll have to speak to her – yes, siree, I'm going to speak right up to her. I may have to be a little harsh, but it's my money runs this house, and I want my share of the profits. No foolishness now. Shell out, I tell you,' the old man whispered, peering out of the corners of his blue, watery eyes at the sleeping form of the young man on the bed.

And now again the old man stood at the door of the room, looking anxiously in. A bell called insistently, announcing that the evening meal was ready to be served, and they went below, Will leading the way. At a long table in the dining-room several men had already gathered, and there was the sound of more footsteps on the stairs.

Two long rows of young workmen eating silently. Saturday night and two long rows of young workmen eating in silence.

After the eating, and on this particular night, there would be a swift flight of all these young men down into the town, down into the lighted parts of the town.

Will sat at his place gripping the sides of his chair.

There were things men did on Saturday nights. Work was at an end for the week and money jingled in pockets. Young workmen ate in silence and hurried away, one by one, down into the town.

Will's sister Kate was going to be married in the spring. Her walking about with the young clerk from the jewellery store, in the streets of Bidwell, had come to something.

Young workmen employed in factories in Erie, Pennsylvania, dressed themselves in their best clothes and walked about in the lighted streets of Erie on Saturday evenings. They went into parks. Some stood talking to girls, while others walked with girls through the streets. And there were still others who went into saloons and had drinks. Men stood talking together at a bar. 'Dang that foreman of mine! I'll bust him in the jaw if he gives me any of his lip.'

There was a young man from Bidwell, sitting at a table in a boarding-house at Erie, Pennsylvania, and before him on a plate was a great pile of meat and potatoes. The room was not very well lighted. It was dark and gloomy, and there were black streaks on the grey wall-paper. Shadows played on the walls. On all sides of the young man sat other young men – eating silently, hurriedly.

Will got abruptly up from the table and started for the door that led into the street, but the others paid no attention to him. If he did not want to eat his meat and potatoes, it made no difference to them. The mistress of the house, the wife of the old cornet player, waited on table when the men ate, but now she had gone away to the kitchen. She was a silent, grim-looking woman, dressed always in a black dress.

To the others in the room – except only the old cornet player – Will's going or staying meant nothing at all. He was a young workman, and at such places young workmen were always going and coming.

A man with broad shoulders and a black moustache, a little older than most of the others, did glance up from his business of eating. He nudged his neighbour, and then made a jerky movement with his thumb over his shoulder. 'The new guy has hooked up quickly, eh?' he said, smiling. 'He can't even wait to eat. Lordy, he's got an early date – some skirt waiting for him.'

At his place, opposite where Will had been seated, the cornet player saw Will go, and his eyes followed, filled with alarm. He had counted on an evening of talk, of speaking to Will about his youth, boasting a little in his gentle hesitating way. Now Will had reached the door that led to the street, and in the old man's eyes tears began to gather. Again his lip trembled. Tears were always gathering in the man's eyes, and his lips trembled at the slightest provocation. It was no wonder he could no longer blow a cornet in a band.

And now Will was outside the house in the darkness and, for the cornet player, the evening was spoiled, the house a deserted empty place. He had intended being very plain in his evening's talk with Will, and wanted particularly to speak of a new attitude he hoped to assume toward his wife, in the matter of money. Talking the whole matter out with Will would give him new courage, make him bolder. Well, if his money had bought the house, that was now a boarding-house, he should have some share in its profits. There must be profits. Why run a boarding-house without profits? The woman he had married was no fool.

Even though a man were old he needed a little money in his pockets. Well, an old man, like himself, has a friend, a young fellow, and now and then he wanted to be able to say to his friend, 'Come on, friend, let's have a glass of beer. I know a good place. Let's have a glass of beer and go to the movies. This is on me.'

The cornet player could not eat his meat and potatoes. For a time he stared over the heads of the others, and then got up to go to his room. His wife followed into the little hallway at the foot of the stairs. 'What's the matter, dearie – are you sick?' she asked.

'No,' he answered, 'I just didn't want any supper.' He did not look at her, but tramped slowly and heavily up the stairs.

Will was walking hurriedly through streets, but did not go down into the brightly lighted sections of town. The boarding-house stood on a factory street and, turning north-ward, he crossed several railroad tracks and went toward the docks, along the shore of Lake Erie. There was some-thing to be settled with himself, something to be faced. Could he manage the matter?

He walked along, hurriedly at first, and then more slowly. It was getting into late October now and there was a sharpness like frost in the air. The spaces between street lamps were long, and he plunged in and out of areas of darkness. Why was it that everything about him seemed suddenly strange and unreal? He had forgotten to bring his overcoat from Bidwell and would have to write Kate to send it.

Now he had almost reached the docks. Not only the night but his own body, the pavements under his feet, and the stars far away in the sky – even the solid factory build-ings he was now passing – seemed strange and unreal. It was almost as though one could thrust out an arm and push a hand through the walls, as one might push his hand into a fog or a cloud of smoke. All the people Will passed seemed strange, and acted in a strange way. Dark figures surged toward him out of the darkness. By a factory wall there was a man standing – perfectly still, motionless. There was something almost unbelievable about the actions of such men and the strangeness of such hours as the one through which he was now passing. He walked within a few inches of the motionless man. Was it a man, or a shadow on the wall? The life Will was now to lead alone had become a strange, a vast, terrifying thing. Perhaps all life was like that, a vastness and emptiness.

He came out into a place where ships were made fast to a dock, and stood for a time facing the high wall-like side of a vessel. It looked dark and deserted. When he turned his head he became aware of a man and a woman passing along a roadway. Their feet made no sound in the thick dust of the roadway, and he could not see or hear them, but knew they were there. Some part of a woman's dress – something white – flashed faintly into view and the man's figure was a dark mass against the dark mass of the night. 'Oh, come on, don't be afraid,' the man whispered hoarsely. 'There won't anything happen to you.'

'Do shut up,' a woman's voice answered, and there was a quick outburst of laughter. The figures fluttered away. 'You don't know what you are talking about,' the woman's voice said again.

Now that he had got Kate's letter, Will was no longer a boy. A boy is, quite naturally, and without his having anything to do with the matter, connected with something – and now that connection had been cut. He had been pushed out of the nest, and that fact, the pushing of himself off the nest's rim, was something accomplished. The difficulty was that, while he was no longer a boy, he had not yet become a man. He was a thing swinging in space. There was no place to put down his feet.

He stood in the darkness under the shadow of the ship, making queer little wriggling motions with his shoulders, that had become now almost the shoulders of a man. No need now to think of evenings at the Appleton house with Kate and Fred standing about, and his father, Tom Appleton, spreading his paint-brushes on the kitchen table; no need of thinking of the sound of Kate's feet going up a stairway of the Appleton house, late at night when she had been out walking with her clerk. What was the good of trying to amuse oneself by thinking of a shepherd dog in an Ohio town, a dog made ridiculous by the trembling hand of a timid old woman?

One stood face to face with manhood now – one stood alone. If only one could get one's feet down upon something, could get over this feeling of falling through space, through a vast emptiness.

'Manhood' – the word had a queer sound in the head. What did it mean?

Will tried to think of himself as a man, doing a man's work in a factory. There was nothing in the factory, where he was now employed, upon which he could put down his feet. All day he stood at a machine and bored holes in pieces of iron. A boy brought to him the little, short, meaningless pieces of iron in a box-like truck, and, one by one, he picked them up and placed them under the point of a drill. He pulled a lever and the drill came down and bit into the pieces of iron. A little smoke-like vapour arose, and then he squirted oil on the spot where the drill was working. Then the lever was thrown up again. The hole was drilled and now the meaningless piece of iron was thrown into another box-like truck. It had nothing to do with him. He had nothing to do with it.

At the noon hour, at the factory, one moved about a bit, stepped outside the factory door to stand for a moment in the sun. Inside, men were sitting along benches, eating lunches out of dinner-pails, and some had washed their hands while others had not bothered about such a trivial matter. They were eating in silence. A tall man spat on the floor and then drew his foot across the spot. Nights came and one went home from the factory to eat, sitting with other silent men, and later a boastful old man came into one's room to talk. One lay on a bed and tried to listen, but presently fell asleep. Men were like the pieces of iron in which holes had been bored – one pitched them aside into a box-like truck. One had nothing really to do with them. They had nothing to do with oneself. Life became a procession of days, and perhaps all life was just like that – just a procession of days.

'Manhood.'

Did one go out of one place and into another? Were youth and manhood two houses, in which one lived during different periods in life? It was evident something of importance must be about to happen to his sister Kate. First, she has been a young woman, having two brothers and a father, living with them in a house at Bidwell, Ohio.

And then a day was to come when she became something else. She married and went to live in another house and had a husband. Perhaps children would be born to her. It was evident Kate had got hold of something, that her hands had reached out and had grasped something definite. Kate had swung herself off the rim of the home nest and, right away, her feet had landed on another limb of the tree of life – womanhood.

As he stood in the darkness something caught at Will's throat. He was fighting again, but what was he fighting? A fellow like himself did not move out of one house and into another. There was a house in which one lived, and then, suddenly and unexpectedly, it fell apart. One stood on the rim of the nest and looked about, and a hand reached out from the warmth of the nest and pushed one off into space. There was no place for a fellow to put down his feet. He was one swinging in space.

What – a great fellow, nearly six feet tall now, and crying in the darkness, in the shadow of a ship, like a child! He walked, filled with determination, out of the darkness, along many streets of factories, and came into a street of houses. He passed a store where groceries were sold and, looking in, saw, by a clock on the wall, that it was already ten o'clock. Two drunken men came out at the door of a house and stood on a little porch. One of them clung to a railing about the porch, and the other pulled at his arm. 'Let me alone. It's settled. I want you to let me alone,' grumbled the man clinging to the railing.

Will went to his boarding-house and climbed the stairs wearily. The devil – one might face anything if one but knew what was to be faced!

He turned on a light and sat down in his room on the edge of the bed, and the old cornet player pounced upon him, pounced like a little animal lying under a bush along a path in a forest, and waiting for food. He came into Will's room carrying his cornet, and there was an almost bold look in his eyes. Standing firmly on his old legs in the centre of the room, he made a declaration. 'I'm going to play it. I don't care what she says, I'm going to play it,' he said.

He put the cornet to his lips and blew two or three notes – so softly that even Will, sitting so closely, could barely hear. Then his eyes wavered. 'My lip's no good,' he said. He thrust the cornet at Will. 'You blow it,' he said.

Will sat on the edge of the bed and smiled. There was a notion floating in his mind now. Was there something, a thought in which one could find comfort? There was now, before him, standing before him in the room, a man who was after all not a man. He was a child, as Will was, too, really, had always been such a child, would always be such a child. One need not be too afraid. Children were all about, everywhere. If one were a child and lost in a vast, empty space, one could at least talk to some other child. One could have conversations, understand perhaps something of the eternal childishness of oneself and others.

Will's thoughts were not very definite. He only felt suddenly warm and comfortable in the little room at the top of the boarding-house.

And now the man was again explaining himself. He wanted to assert his manhood. 'I stay up here,' he explained, 'and don't go down there to sleep in the room with my wife because I don't want to. That's the only reason. I could if I wanted to. She has the bronchitis – but don't tell anyone. Women hate to have anyone told. She isn't so bad. I can do what I please.'

He kept urging Will to put the cornet to his lips and blow. There was in him an intense eagerness. 'You can't really make any music – you don't know how – but that don't make any difference,' he said. 'The thing to do is to make a noise, make a deuce of a racket, blow like the devil.'

Again Will felt like crying, but the sense of vastness and loneliness that had been in him since he got aboard the train that night at Bidwell had gone. 'Well, I can't go on for ever being a baby. Kate has a right to get married,' he thought, putting the cornet to his lips. He blew two or three notes, softly.

'No, I tell you, no! That isn't the way! Blow on it!

Don't be afraid! I tell you I want you to do it. Make a deuce of a racket! I tell you what, I own this house. We don't need to be afraid. We can do what we please. Go ahead! Make a deuce of a racket!' the old man kept pleading.

THE MAN'S STORY

*

DURING his trial for murder, and later, after he had been cleared through the confession of that queer little bald chap with the nervous hands, I watched him, fascinated by his continued effort to make something understood.

He was persistently interested in something, having nothing to do with the charge that he had murdered the woman. The matter of whether or not, and by due process of law, he was to be convicted of murder and hanged by the neck until he was dead didn't seem to interest him. The law was something outside his life and he declined to have anything to do with the killing as one might decline a cigarette. 'I thank you, I am not smoking at present. I made a bet with a fellow that I could go along without smoking cigarettes for a month.'

That is the sort of thing I mean. It was puzzling. Really, had he been guilty and trying to save his neck, he couldn't have taken a better line. You see, at first everyone thought he had done the killing; we were all convinced of it; and then, just because of that magnificent air of indifference, everyone began wanting to save him. When news came of the confession of the crazy little stage-hand everyone broke out into cheers.

He was clear of the law after that, but his manner in no way changed. There was, somewhere, a man or a woman who would understand just what he understood, and it was important to find that person and talk things over. There was a time, during the trial and immediately afterward, when I saw a good deal of him, and I had this sharp sense of him, feeling about in the darkness trying to find something like a needle or a pin lost on the floor. Well, he was

166

like an old man who cannot find his glasses. He feels in all his pockets and looks helplessly about.

There was a question in my mind, too, in everyone's mind – 'Can a man be wholly casual and brutal, in every outward way, at a moment when the one nearest and dearest to him is dying, and at the same time, and with quite another part of himself, be altogether tender and sensitive?'

Anyway, it's a story, and once in a while a man likes to tell a story straight out, without putting in any newspaper jargon about beautiful heiresses, cold-blooded murderers and all that sort of tommyrot.

As I picked the story up the sense of it was something like this:

The man's name was Wilson – Edgar Wilson – and he had come to Chicago from some place to the westward, perhaps from the mountains. He might once have been a sheep-herder or something of the sort in the far west, as he had the peculiar abstract air, acquired only by being a good deal alone. About himself and his past he told a good many conflicting stories, and so, after being with him for a time, one instinctively discarded the past.

'The devil – it doesn't matter – the man can't tell the truth in that direction – Let it go,' one said to oneself. What was known was that he had come to Chicago from a town in Kansas, and that he had run away from the Kansas town with another man's wife.

As to her story, I knew little enough of it. She had been at one time, I imagine, a rather handsome thing, in a big, strong, upstanding sort of way, but her life, until she met Wilson, had been rather messy. In those dead flat

Kansas towns lives have a way of getting ugly and messy without anything very definite having happened to make them so. One can't imagine the reasons – Let it go. It just is so, and one can't at all believe the writers of Western tales about the life out there. .

To be a little more definite about this particular woman – in her young girlhood her father had got into trouble. He had been some sort of a small official, a travelling agent or something of the sort for an express company, and got arrested in connection with the disappearance of some money. And then, when he was in jail and before his trial, he shot and killed himself. The girl's mother was already dead.

Within a year or two she married a man, an honest enough fellow, but from all accounts rather uninteresting. He was a drug clerk and a frugal man, and after a short time managed to buy a drug store of his own.

The woman, as I have said, had been strong and well-built, but now grew thin and nervous. Still, she carried herself well, with a sort of air, as it were, and there was something about her that appealed strongly to men. Several men of the seedy little town were smitten by her and wrote her letters, trying to get her to creep out with them at night. You know how such things are done. The letters were unsigned. 'You go to such and such a place on Friday evening. If you are willing to talk things over with me, carry a book in your hand.'

Then the woman made a mistake and told her husband about the receipt of one of the letters, and he grew angry and tramped off to the trysting-place at night with a shotgun in his hand. When no one appeared he came home and fussed about. He said little mean, tentative things. 'You must have looked – in a certain way – at the man when he passed you on the street. A man don't grow so bold with a married woman unless an opening has been given him.'

The man talked and talked after that, and life in the house must have been gay. She grew habitually silent, and when she was silent the house was silent. They had no children.

Then the man Edgar Wilson came along, going eastward, and stopped over in the town for two or three days. He had at that time a little money and stayed at a small working-men's boarding-house near the railroad station. One day he saw the woman walking in the street and followed her to her home, and the neighbours saw them standing and talking together for an hour by the front gate, and on the next day he came again.

That time they talked for two hours; and then she went into the house, got a few belongings and walked to the railroad station with him. They took a train for Chicago and lived there together, apparently very happy, until she died – in a way I am about to try to tell you about. They, of course, could not be married, and during the three years they lived in Chicago he did nothing toward earning their common living. As he had a very small amount of money when they came, barely enough to get them here from the Kansas town, they were miserably poor.

They lived, when I knew about them, over on the North side, in that section of old three- and four-story brick residences that were once the homes of what we call our nice people, but that had afterward gone to the bad. The section is having a kind of re-birth now, but for a good many years it rather went to seed. There were these old residences, made into boarding-houses, and with unbelievably dirty lace curtains at the windows, and now and then an utterly disreputable old tumble-down frame-house – in one of which Wilson lived with his woman.

The place is a sight! Someone owns it, I suppose, who is shrewd enough to know that in a big city like Chicago no section gets neglected always. Such a fellow must have said to himself, 'Well, I'll let the place go. The ground on which the house stands will some day be very valuable, but the house is worth nothing. I'll let it go at a low rental and do nothing to fix it up. Perhaps I will get enough out of it to pay my taxes until prices come up.'

And so the house had stood there unpainted for years, and the windows were out of line and the shingles nearly all off the roof. The second floor was reached by an outside stairway with a handrail that had become just the peculiar grey greasy black that wood can become in a soft-coal-burning city like Chicago or Pittsburg. One's hand became black when the railing was touched, and the rooms above were altogether cold and cheerless.

At the front there was a large room with a fireplace, from which many bricks had fallen, and back of that were two small sleeping-rooms.

Wilson and his woman lived in the place, at the time when the thing happened I am to tell you about, and as they had taken it in May I presume they did not too much mind the cold barrenness of the large front room in which they lived. There was a sagging wooden bed with a leg broken off – the woman had tried to repair it with sticks from a packing-box – a kitchen table, that was also used by Wilson as a writing-desk, and two or three cheap kitchen chairs.

The woman had managed to get a place as wardrobe

woman in a theatre in Randolph Street and they lived on
her earnings. It was said she had got the job because
some man connected with the theatre, or a company playing there, had a passion for her; but one can always pick
up stories of that sort about any woman who works about
the theatre – from the scrubwoman to the star.

Anyway, she worked there, and had a reputation in the
theatre of being quiet and efficient.

As for Wilson, he wrote poetry of a sort I've never seen
before, although, like most newspaper men, I've taken a
turn at verse-making myself now and then – both of the
rhymed kind and the new-fangled *vers libre* sort. I rather
go in for the classical stuff myself.

About Wilson's verse – it was Greek to me. Well now,
to get right down to hardpan in this matter, it was and it
wasn't.

The stuff made me feel just a little bit woozy when I
took a whole sheaf of it and sat alone in my room reading
it at night. It was all about walls, and deep wells, and
great bowls with young trees standing erect in them – and
trying to find their way to the light and air over the rim of
the bowl.

Queer, crazy stuff, every line of it, but fascinating too –
in a way. One got into a new world with new values,
which after all is, I suppose, what poetry is all about.
There was the world of fact – we all know, or think we
know – the world of flat buildings and middle-western
farms with wire fences about the fields and Fordson tractors
running up and down, and towns with high schools and
advertising billboards, and everything that makes up life –
or that we think makes up life.

There was this world we all walk about in, and then

there was this other world, that I have come to think of as Wilson's world – a dim place to me at least – of far-away near places – things taking new and strange shapes, the insides of peoples coming out, the eyes seeing new things, the fingers feeling new and strange things.

It was a place of walls mainly. I got hold of the whole lot of Wilson's verse by a piece of luck. It happened that I was the first newspaper man who got into the place on the night when the woman's body was found, and there was all his stuff, carefully written out in a sort of child's copy-book, and two or three stupid policemen standing about. I just shoved the book under my coat, when they weren't looking, and later, during Wilson's trial, we published some of the more intelligible ones in the paper. It made pretty good newspaper stuff – the poet who killed his mistress,

> 'He did not wear his purple coat,
> For blood and wine are red' –

and all that. Chicago loved it.

To get back to the poetry itself for a moment. I just wanted to explain that all through the book there ran this notion, that men had erected walls about themselves and that all men were perhaps destined to stand for ever behind the walls – on which they constantly beat with their fists, or with whatever tools they could get hold of. Wanted to break through to something, you understand. One couldn't quite make out whether there was just one great wall or many little individual walls. Sometimes Wilson put it one way, sometimes another. Men had themselves built the walls and now stood behind them, knowing dimly that beyond the walls there was warmth, light, air, beauty, life, in fact — while at the same time, and because of a kind of madness in themselves, the walls were constantly being built higher and stronger.

The notion gives you the fantods a little, doesn't it? Anyway, it does me.

And then there was that notion about deep wells, men everywhere constantly digging and digging themselves down deeper and deeper into deep wells. They not wanting to do it, you understand, and no one wanting them to do it, but all the time the thing going on just the same; that is to say, the wells getting constantly deeper and deeper, and the voices growing dimmer and dimmer in the distance — and again the light and the warmth of life going away and going away, because of a kind of blind refusal of people to try to understand each other, I suppose.

It was all very strange to me — Wilson's poetry, I mean — when I came to it. Here is one of his things. It is not directly concerned with the walls, the bowl or the deep well theme, as you will see, but it is one we ran in the paper during the trial, and a lot of folks rather liked it — as I'll admit I do myself. Maybe putting it in here will give a kind of point to my story, by giving you some sense of the strangeness of the man who is the story's hero. In the book it was called merely 'Number Ninety-seven,' and it went as follows:

'The firm grip of my fingers on the thin paper of this cigarette is a sign that I am very quiet now. Sometimes it is not so. When I am unquiet I am weak, but when I am quiet, as I am now, I am very strong.

'Just now I went along one of the streets of my city and in at a door and came up here, where I am now, lying on a bed and looking out at a window. Very suddenly and completely the knowledge has come to me that I could grip the sides of tall buildings as freely and as easily as I now grip this cigarette. I could hold the building between my fingers, put it to my lips and blow smoke through it. I could blow confusion away. I could blow a thousand people out through the roof of one tall building into the sky, into the unknown. Building after building I could consume, as I consume the cigarettes in this box. I could throw the burning ends of cities over my shoulder and out through a window.

'It is not often I get in the state I am now in – so quiet and sure of myself. When the feeling comes over me there is a directness and simplicity in me that makes me love myself. To myself at such times I say strong sweet words.

'I am on a couch by this window, and I could ask a woman to come here to lie with me, or a man either for that matter.

'I could take a row of houses standing on a street, tip them over, empty the people out of them, squeeze and compress all the people into one person and love that person.

'Do you see this hand? Suppose it held a knife that could cut down through all the falseness in you. Suppose it could cut down through the sides of buildings and houses where thousands of people now lie asleep.

'It would be something worth thinking about if the fingers of this hand gripped a knife that could cut and rip through all the ugly husks in which millions of lives are enclosed.'

174

Well, there is the idea, you see, a kind of power that could be tender too. I will quote you just one more of his things, a more gentle one. It is called in the book, 'Number Eighty-three.'

'I am a tree that grows beside the wall. I have been thrusting up and up. My body is covered with scars. My body is old, but still I thrust upward, creeping toward the top of the wall.

'It is my desire to drop blossoms and fruit over the wall.

'I would moisten dry lips.

'I would drop blossoms on the heads of children, over the top of the wall.

'I would caress with falling blossoms the bodies of those who live on the further side of the wall.

'My branches are creeping upward and new sap comes into me out of the dark ground under the wall.

'My fruit shall not be my fruit until it drops from my arms, into the arms of the others, over the top of the wall.'

And now as to the life led by the man and woman in the large upper room in that old frame-house. By a stroke of luck I have recently got rather a line on that by a discovery I have made.

After they had moved into the house – it was only last spring – the theatre in which the woman was employed was dark for a long time and they were more than usually hard up, so the woman tried to pick up a little extra money

– to help pay the rent, I suppose – by subletting the two little back rooms of that place of theirs.

Various people lived in the dark tiny holes, just how I can't make out, as there was no furniture. Still there are places in Chicago, called 'flops,' where one may sleep on the floor for five or ten cents, and they are more patronized than respectable people know anything about.

What I did discover was a little woman – she wasn't so young, but she was hunchbacked and small, and it is hard not to think of her as a girl – who once lived in one of the rooms for several weeks. She had a job as ironer in a small hand-laundry in the neighbourhood and someone had given her a cheap folding cot. She was a curiously sentimental creature, with the kind of hurt eyes deformed people often have, and I have a fancy she had herself a romantic attach-ment of a sort for the man Wilson. Anyway, I managed to find out a lot from her.

After the other woman's death, and after Wilson had been cleared on the murder charge, by the confession of the stage-hand, I used to go over to the house where he had lived, sometimes in the late afternoon after our paper had been put to bed for the day. Ours is an afternoon paper and after two o'clock most of us are free.

I found the hunchback girl standing in front of the house one day and began talking with her. She was a gold-mine.

There was that look in her eyes I've told you of, the hurt, sensitive look. I just spoke to her and we began talking of Wilson. She had lived in one of the rooms at the back. She told me of that at once.

On some days she found herself unable to work at the laundry because her strength suddenly gave out, and so, on such days, she stayed in the room, lying on the cot. Blinding headaches came that lasted for hours, during which she was almost entirely unconscious of everything going on about her. Then afterwards she was quite conscious, but for a long time very weak. She wasn't one who is destined to live very long, I suppose, and I presume she didn't much care.

Anyway, there she was in the room, in that weak state after the times of illness, and she grew curious about the two people in the front room, so she used to get off her couch and go softly in her stockinged feet to the door between the rooms and peep through the keyhole. She had to kneel on the dusty floor to do it.

The life in the room fascinated her from the beginning. Sometimes the man was in there alone, sitting at the kitchen table and writing the stuff he afterward put into the book I collared, and from which I have quoted; sometimes the woman was with him, and again sometimes he was in there alone but wasn't writing. Then he was always walking and walking up and down.

When both people were in the room, and when the man was writing, the woman seldom moved, but sat in a chair by one of the windows with her hands crossed. He would write a few lines and then walk up and down talking to himself or to her. When he spoke she did not answer, except with her eyes, the crippled girl said. What I gathered of all this from her talk with me, and what is the product of my own imaginings, I confess I do not quite know.

Anyway, what I got and what I am trying, in my own way, to transmit to you is a sense of a kind of strangeness in the relationship of the two. It wasn't just a domestic household, a little down on its luck, by any means. He was trying to do something very difficult – with his poetry, I presume – and she in her own way was trying to help him.

And of course, as I have no doubt you have gathered from what I have quoted of Wilson's verse, the matter had something to do with the relationships between people – not necessarily between the particular man and woman who happened to be there in that room, but between all peoples.

The fellow had some half-mystic conception of all such things and, before he found his own woman, had been going aimlessly about the world looking for a mate. Then he had found the woman in the Kansas town and – he at least thought – things had cleared, for him.

Well, he had the notion that no one in the world could think or feel anything alone, and that people only got into trouble and walled themselves in by trying it, or something of the sort. There was a discord. Things were jangled. Someone, it seems, had to strike a pitch that all voices could take up before the real song of life could begin. Mind you, I'm not putting forth any notions of my own. What I am trying to do is to give you a sense of something I got from having read Wilson's stuff, from having known him a little, and from having seen something of the effect of his personality upon others.

He felt, quite definitely, that no one in the world could feel or even think alone. And then there was the notion that, if one tried to think with the mind without taking the body into account, one got all balled-up. True conscious life built itself up like a pyramid. First the body and mind of a beloved one must come into one's thinking and feeling, and then, in some mystic way, the bodies and minds of all the other people in the world must come in, must

178

come sweeping in like a great wind — or something of the sort.

Is all this a little tangled up to you, who read my story of Wilson? It may not be. It may be that your minds are more clear than my own and that what I take to be so difficult will be very simple to you.

However, I have to bring up to you just what I can find, after diving down into this sea of motives and impulses — I admit I don't rightly understand.

The hunchback girl felt (or is it my own fancy colouring what she said?) — it doesn't really matter. The thing to get at is what the man Edgar Wilson felt.

He felt, I fancy, that in the field of poetry he had something to express that could never be expressed until he had found a woman who could, in a peculiar and absolute way, give herself in the world of the flesh — and that then there was to be a marriage out of which beauty would come for all people. He had to find the woman who had that power, and the power had to be untainted by self-interest, I fancy. A profound egotist, you see — and he thought he had found what he needed in the wife of the Kansas druggist.

He had found her and had done something to her. What it was I can't quite make out, except that she was absolutely and wholly happy with him, in a strangely inexpressive sort of way.

Trying to speak of him and his influence on others is rather like trying to walk on a tight-rope stretched between two tall buildings above a crowded street. A cry from below, a laugh, the honk of an automobile horn, and down one goes into nothingness. One simply becomes ridiculous.

He wanted, it seems, to condense the flesh and the spirit

of himself and his woman into his poems. You will remember that in one of the things of his I have quoted he
speaks of condensing, of squeezing all the people of a city
into one person and of loving that person.

One might think of him as a powerful person, almost
hideously powerful. You will see, as you read, how he has
got me in his power and is making me serve his purpose.

And he had caught and was holding the woman in his
grip. He had wanted her – quite absolutely, and had taken
her – as all men, perhaps, want to do with their women,
and don't quite dare. Perhaps, too, she was in her own way
greedy, and he was making actual love to her always day
and night, when they were together and when they were
apart.

I'll admit I am confused about the whole matter myself.
I am trying to express something I have felt, not in myself,
nor in the words that came to me from the lips of the
hunchback girl, whom, you will remember, I left kneeling
on the floor in that back room and peeping through a keyhole.

There she was, you see, the hunchback, and in the room
before her were the man and woman, and the hunchback
girl also had fallen under the power of the man Wilson.
She also was in love with him – there can be no doubt of
that. The room in which she knelt was dark and dusty.
There must have been a thick accumulation of dust on the
floor.

What she said – or if she did not say the words, what
she made me feel was that the man Wilson worked in the
room, or walked up and down in there before his woman,
and that, while he did that, his woman sat in the chair, and
that there was in her face, in her eyes, a look –

He was all the time making love to her, and his making love to her in just that abstract way was a kind of love-making with all people; and that was possible because the woman was as purely physical as he was something else. If all this is meaningless to you, at least it wasn't to the hunchback girl – who certainly was uneducated and never would have set herself up as having any special powers of understanding. She knelt in the dust, listening, and look-ing in at the keyhole, and in the end she came to feel that the man, in whose presence she had never been and whose person had never in any way touched her person, had made love to her also.

She had felt that, and it had gratified her entire nature. One might say it had satisfied her. She was what she was and it had made life worth living for her.

Minor things happened in the room and one may speak of them.

For example, there was a day in June, a dark, warm, rainy day. The hunchback girl was in her room, kneeling on the floor, and Wilson and his woman were in their room.

Wilson's woman had been doing a family washing, and, as it could not be dried outdoors, she had stretched ropes across the room and had hung the clothes inside.

When the clothes were all hung, Wilson came from walking outside in the rain and, going to the desk, sat down and began to write.

He wrote for a few minutes and then got up and went about the room, and in walking a wet garment brushed against his face.

He kept right on walking and talking to the woman, but

as he walked and talked he gathered all the clothes in his
arms and going to the little landing at the head of the stairs
outside, threw them down into the muddy yard below. He
did that and the woman sat without moving or saying
anything until he had gone back to his desk; then she went
down the stairs, got the clothes and washed them again –
and it was only after she had done that, and when she was
again hanging them in the room above, that he appeared to
know what he had done.

While the clothes were being re-washed he went for
another walk, and when she heard his footsteps on the
stairs the hunchback girl ran to the keyhole. As she knelt
there, and as he came into the room, she could look
directly into his face. 'He was like a puzzled child for a
moment, and then, although he said nothing, the tears
began to run down his cheeks,' she said. That happened,
and then the woman, who was at the moment re-hanging
the clothes, turned and saw him. She had her arm filled
with clothes, but dropped them on the floor and ran to him.
She half-knelt, the hunchback girl said, and putting her
arms about his body and looking up into his face pleaded
with him. 'Don't. Don't be hurt. Believe me, I know
everything. Please don't be hurt,' was what she said.

And now as to the story of the woman's death. It happened in the fall of that year.

In the place where she was sometimes employed – that
is to say, in the theatre – there was this other man, the little
half-crazed stage-hand who shot her.

He had fallen in love with her and, like the men in the
Kansas town from which she came, had written her
several silly notes of which she said nothing to Wilson.

The letters weren't very nice, and some of them, the most unpleasant ones, were, by some twist of the fellow's mind, signed with Wilson's name. Two of them were afterwards found on her person and were brought in as evidence against Wilson during his trial.

And so the woman worked in the theatre and the summer had passed, and on an evening in the fall there was to be a dress-rehearsal at the theatre, and the woman went there, taking Wilson with her. It was a fall day, such as we sometimes have in Chicago, cold and wet and with a heavy fog lying over the city.

The dress-rehearsal did not come off. The star was ill, or something of the sort happened, and Wilson and his woman sat about in the cold empty theatre for an hour or two, and then the woman was told she could go for the night.

She and Wilson walked across the city, stopping to get something to eat at a small restaurant. He was in one of the abstract silent moods common to him. No doubt he was thinking of the things he wanted to express in the poetry I have tried to tell you about. He went along, not seeing the woman beside him, not seeing the people drifting up to them and passing them in the streets. He went along in that way and she —

She was, no doubt, then as she always was in his presence — silent and satisfied with the fact that she was with him. There was nothing he could think or feel that did not take her into account. The very blood flowing up through his body was her blood too. He had made her feel that, and she was silent and satisfied as he went along, his body walking beside her, but his fancy groping its way through the land of high walls and deep wells.

183

They had walked from the restaurant, in the Loop District, over a bridge to the North Side, and still no words passed between them.

When they had almost reached their own place the stage-hand, the small man with the nervous hands who had written the notes, appeared out of the fog, as though out of nowhere, and shot the woman.

That was all there was to it. It was as simple as that.

They were walking as I have described them, when a head flashed up before the woman in the midst of the fog, a hand shot out, there was the quick abrupt sound of a pistol-shot, and then the absurd little stage-hand, he with the wrinkled, impotent little old woman's face – then he turned and ran away.

All that happened just as I have written it, and it made no impression at all on the mind of Wilson. He walked along as though nothing had happened and the woman, after half-falling, gathered herself together and managed to continue walking beside him, still saying nothing.

They went thus for perhaps two blocks, and had reached the foot of the outer stairs that led up to their place when a policeman came running, and the woman told him a lie. She told him some story about a struggle between two drunken men, and after a moment of talk the policeman went away, sent away by the woman in a direction opposite to the one taken by the fleeing stage-hand.

They were in the darkness and the fog now, and the woman took her man's arm while they climbed the stairs. He was as yet – as far as I will ever be able to explain logically – unaware of the shot, and of the fact that she was dying, although he had seen and heard everything.

184

What the doctors said, who were put on the case afterwards was that a cord or muscle, or something of the sort that controls the action of the heart, had been practically severed by the shot.

She was dead and alive at the same time, I should say.

Anyway, the two people marched up the stairs and into the room above, and then a really dramatic and lovely thing happened. One wishes that the scene, with just all its connotations, could be played out on a stage instead of having to be put down in words.

The two came into the room, the one dead but not ready to acknowledge death without a flash of something individual and lovely, that is to say, the one dead while still alive, and the other alive but at the moment dead to what was going on.

The room into which they went was dark, but, with the sure instinct of an animal, the woman walked across the room to the fireplace, while the man stopped and stood some ten feet from the door – thinking and thinking in his peculiarly abstract way. The fireplace was filled with an accumulation of waste matter, cigarette-ends – the man was a hard smoker – bits of paper on which he had scribbled – the rubbishy accumulation that gathers about all such fellows as Wilson. There was all of this quickly combustible material stuffed into the fireplace on this – the first cold evening of the fall.

And so the woman went to it, and found a match somewhere in the darkness, and touched the pile off.

There is a picture that will remain with me always – just that – the barren room and the blind, unseeing man standing there, and the woman kneeling and making a little flare of beauty at the last. Little flames leaped up.

Lights crept and danced over the walls. Below, on the
floor of the room, there was a deep well of darkness in
which the man, blind with his own purpose, was standing.

The pile of burning papers must have made, for a
moment, quite a glare of light in the room, and the woman
stood for a moment beside the fireplace, just outside the
glare of light.

And then, pale and wavering, she walked across the light,
as across a lighted stage, going softly and silently toward
him. Had she also something to say? No one will ever
know. What happened was that she said nothing.

She walked across to him and, at the moment she
reached him, fell down on the floor and died at his feet,
and at the same moment the little fire of papers died. If
she struggled before she died, there on the floor, she
struggled in silence. There was no sound. She had fallen
and lay between him and the door that led out to the stairway and to the street.

It was then Wilson became altogether inhuman – too
much so for my understanding.

The fire had died and the woman he had loved had died.

And there he stood looking into nothingness, thinking
– God knows – perhaps of nothingness.

He stood a minute, five minutes, perhaps ten. He was
a man who, before he found the woman, had been sunk
far down into a deep sea of doubt and questionings. Before
he found the woman no expression had ever come from
him. He had perhaps just wandered from place to place,
looking at people's faces, wondering about people, wanting
to come close to others and not knowing how. The
woman had been able to lift him up to the surface of the

sea of life for a time, and with her he had floated on the surface of the sea, under the sky, in the sunlight. The woman's warm body – given to him in love – had been as a boat in which he had floated on the surface of the sea, and now the boat had been wrecked and he was sinking again, back into the sea.

All of this had happened and he did not know – that is to say he did not know, and at the same time he did know.

He was a poet, I presume, and perhaps at the moment a new poem was forming itself in his mind.

At any rate, he stood for a time, as I have said, and then he must have had a feeling that he should make some move, that he should, if possible, save himself from some disaster about to overtake him.

He had an impulse to go to the door, and by way of the stairway to go downstairs and into the street – but the body of the woman was between him and the door.

What he did, and what, when he later told of it, sounded so terribly cruel to others, was to treat the woman's dead body as one might treat a fallen tree in the darkness in a forest. First he tried to push the body aside with his foot, and then, as that seemed impossible, he stepped awkwardly over it.

He stepped directly on the woman's arm. The discoloured mark where his heel landed was afterwards found on the body.

He almost fell, and then his body righted itself and he went walking, marched down the rickety stairs and went walking in the streets.

By chance the night had cleared. It had grown colder and a cold wind had driven the fog away. He walked along, very nonchalantly, for several blocks. He walked along as calmly as you, the reader, might walk, after having had lunch with a friend.

As a matter of fact, he even stopped to make a purchase at a store. I remember that the place was called 'The Whip.' He went in, bought himself a package of cigarettes, lighted one and stood a moment, apparently listening to a conversation going on among several idlers in the place.

And then he strolled again, going along smoking the cigarette and thinking of his poem, no doubt. Then he came to a moving-picture theatre.

That perhaps touched him off. He also was an old fireplace, stuffed with old thoughts, scraps of unwritten poems – God knows what rubbish! Often he had gone at night to the theatre where the woman was employed to walk home with her, and now the people were coming out of a small moving-picture house. They had been in there seeing a play called 'The Light of the World.'

Wilson walked into the midst of the crowd, lost himself in the crowd, smoking his cigarette, and then he took off his hat, looked anxiously about for a moment, and suddenly began shouting in a loud voice.

He stood there, shouting and trying to tell the story of what had happened in a loud voice, and with the uncertain air of one trying to remember a dream. He did that for a moment, and then, after running a little way along the pavement, stopped and began his story again. It was only after he had gone thus, in short rushes, back along the street to the house and up the rickety stairway to where the woman was lying – the crowd following curiously at his heels – that a policeman came up and arrested him.

He seemed excited at first, but was quiet afterwards, and

he laughed at the notion of insanity when the lawyer who had been retained for him tried to set up the plea in court.

As I have said, his action during his trial was confusing to us all, as he seemed wholly uninterested in the murder and in his own fate. After the confession of the man who had fired the shot, he seemed to feel no resentment toward him either. There was something he wanted, having nothing to do with what had happened.

There he had been, you see, before he found the woman, wandering about in the world, digging himself deeper and deeper into the deep wells he talked about in his poetry, building the wall between himself and all us others constantly higher and higher.

He knew what he was doing, but he could not stop. That's what he kept talking about, pleading with people about. The man had come up out of the sea of doubt, had grasped for a time the hand of the woman, and with her hand in his had floated for a time upon the surface of life – but now he felt himself again sinking down into the sea.

His talking and talking, stopping people in the street and talking, going into people's houses and talking, was, I presume, but an effort; he was always afterwards making not to sink back for ever into the sea; it was the struggle of a drowning man, I dare say.

At any rate, I have told you the man's story – have been compelled to try to tell you his story. There was a kind of power in him, and the power has been exerted over me as it was exerted over the woman from Kansas and the unknown hunchback girl, kneeling on the floor in the dust and peering through a keyhole.

Ever since the woman died we have all been trying and trying to drag the man Wilson back out of the sea of doubt and dumbness into which we feel him sinking deeper and deeper — and to no avail.

It may be I have been impelled to tell his story in the hope that by writing of him I may myself understand. Is there not a possibility that with understanding would come also the strength to thrust an arm down into the sea and drag the man Wilson back to the surface again?

AN OHIO PAGAN

*

CHAPTER I

TOM EDWARDS was a Welshman, born in Northern Ohio, and a descendant of that Thomas Edwards, the Welsh poet, who was called, in his own time and country, Twn O'r Nant – which in our own tongue means 'Tom of the dingle or vale.'

The first Thomas Edwards was a gigantic figure in the history of the spiritual life of the Welsh. Not only did he write many stirring interludes concerning life, death, earth, fire and water, but as a man he was a true brother to the elements and to all the passions of his sturdy and musical race. He sang beautifully, but he also played stoutly and beautifully the part of a man. There is a wonderful tale, told in Wales and written into a book by the poet himself, of how he, with a team of horses, once moved a great ship out of the land into the sea, after three hundred Welshmen had failed at the task. Also, he taught Welsh woodsmen the secret of the crane and pulley for lifting great logs in the forests, and once he fought to the point of death the bully of the country-side, a man known over a great part of Wales as The Cruel Fighter. Tom Edwards, the descendant of this man, was born in Ohio, near my own native town of Bidwell. His name was not Edwards, but as his father was dead when he was born, his mother gave him the old poet's name out of pride in having such blood in her veins. Then when the boy was six his mother died also, and the man for whom both his mother and father had worked, a sporting farmer named Harry Whitehead, took the boy into his own house to live.

They were gigantic people, the Whiteheads. Harry himself weighed two hundred and seventy pounds and his wife twenty pounds more. About the time he took young Tom to live with him the farmer became interested in the racing of horses, moved off his farms, of which he had three, and came to live in our town.

In the town of Bidwell there was an old frame-building that had once been a factory for the making of barrel-staves, but that had stood for years vacant, staring with window-less eyes into the streets, and Harry bought it at a low price and transformed it into a splendid stable with a board floor and two long rows of box-stalls. At a sale of blooded horses held in the city of Cleveland he bought twenty young colts, all of the trotting strain, and set up as a trainer of race-horses.

Among the colts thus brought to our town was one great black fellow named Bucephalus. Harry got the name from John Telfer, our town poetry-lover. 'It was the name of the mighty horse of a mighty man,' Telfer said, and that satisfied Harry.

Young Tom was told off to be the special guardian and caretaker of Bucephalus, and the black stallion, who had in him the mighty blood of the Tennessee Patchens, quickly became the pride of the stables. He was in his nature a great ugly-tempered beast, as given to whims and notions as an opera star, and from the very first began to make trouble. Within a year no one but Harry White-head himself and the boy Tom dared go into his stall. The methods of the two people with the great horse were entirely different, but equally effective. Once big Harry turned the stallion loose on the floor of the stable, closed all the doors and, with a cruel long whip in his hand, went in to conquer or to be conquered. He came out victorious, and ever after the horse behaved when he was about.

The boy's method was different. He loved Bucephalus and the wicked animal loved him. Tom slept on a cot in the barn, and day or night, even when there were mares about, walked into Bucephalus' box-stall without fear. When the stallion was in a temper he sometimes turned at the boy's entrance and with a snort sent his iron-shod heels banging against the sides of the stall; but Tom laughed and, putting a simple rope halter over the horse's head, led him forth to be cleaned or hitched to a cart for his morning's jog on our town's half-mile race-track. A sight it was to see the boy with the blood of Twn O'r Nant in his veins leading by the nose Bucephalus of the royal blood of the Patchens.

When he was six years old the horse Bucephalus went forth to race and conquer at the great spring race-meeting at Columbus, Ohio. He won two heats of the trotting free-for-all – the great race of the meeting – with heavy Harry in the sulky and then faltered. A gelding named 'Light o' the Orient' beat him in the next heat. Tom, then a lad of sixteen, was put into the sulky, and the two of them, horse and boy, fought out a royal battle with the gelding and a little bay mare, that hadn't been heard from before, but that suddenly developed a whirlwind burst of speed.

The big stallion and the slender boy won. From amid a mob of cursing, shouting, whip-slashing men a black horse shot out, and a pale boy, leaning far forward, called and murmured to him. 'Go on, boy! Go, boy! Go, boy!' the lad's voice had called over and over all through the race. Bucephalus got a record of 2·06¼ and Tom Edwards became a newspaper hero. His picture was in the Cleveland *Leader* and the Cincinnati *Enquirer*, and when he came back to Bidwell we other boys fairly wept in our envy of him.

Then it was, however, that Tom Edwards fell down from his high place. There he was, a tall boy, almost of man's stature, and, except for a few months during the winters when he lived on the Whitehead farms, and between his sixth and thirteenth years, when he had attended a country school and had learned to read and write and do sums, he was without education. And now, during that very fall of the year of his triumph at Columbus, the Bidwell truant officer, a thin man with white hair, who was also superintendent of the Baptist Sunday School, came one afternoon to the Whitehead stables and told him that if he did not begin going to school both he and his employer would get into serious trouble.

Harry Whitehead was furious, and so was Tom. There he was, a great, tall, slender fellow who had been with race-horses to the fairs all over Northern Ohio and Indiana during that very fall, and who had just come home from the journey during which he had driven the winner in the free-for-all trot at a Grand Circuit meeting and had given Bucephalus a mark of 2·06¼.

Was such a fellow to go sit in a schoolroom, with a silly school-book in his hand, reading of the affairs of the men who dealt in butter, eggs, potatoes and apples, and whose unnecessarily complicated business life the children were asked to unravel — was such a fellow to go sit in a room, under the eyes of a woman teacher, and in the company of boys half his age and with none of his wide experience of life?

It was a hard thought, and Tom took it hard. The law was all right, Harry Whitehead said, and was intended to keep no-account kids off the streets, but what it had to do with himself Tom couldn't make out. When the truant officer had gone and Tom was left alone in the stable with his employer, the man and boy stood for a long time glumly staring at each other. It was all right to be educated, but Tom felt he had book-education enough. He could read, write and do sums, and what other book-training did a horseman need? As for books, they were all right for rainy evenings, when there were no men sitting by the stable door and talking of horses and races. And also when one went to the races in a strange town and arrived, perhaps, on Sunday, and the races did not begin until the following Wednesday – it was all right then to have a book in the chest with the horse-blankets. When the weather was fine and the work was all done on a fine fall afternoon, and the other swipes, both niggers and whites, had gone off to town, one could take a book out under a tree and read of life in far-away places that was as strange, and almost as fascinating, as one's own life. Tom had read *Robinson Crusoe*, *Uncle Tom's Cabin*, and *Tales from the Bible*, all of which he had found in the Whitehead house, and Jacob Friedman, the school superintendent at Bidwell, who had a fancy for horses, had loaned him other books that he intended reading during the coming winter. They were in his chest – one called *Gulliver's Travels* and the other *Moll Flanders*.

And now the law said he must give up being a horseman and go every day to a school and do little foolish sums, he who had already proved himself a man. What other schoolboy knew what he did about life? Had he not seen and spoken to several of the greatest men of this world, men who had driven horses to beat world records, and did they not respect him? When he became a driver of race-horses, such men as Pop Geers, Walter Cox, John Splan, Murphy and the others would not ask him what books he had read, or how many feet make a rod, and how many rods in a mile. In the race at Columbus, where he had won his spurs as a driver, he had already proved that life had given him the kind of education he needed. The driver of the gelding 'Light o' the Orient' had tried to bluff him in that third heat and had not succeeded. He was a big man with a black moustache, and had lost one eye, so that he looked fierce and ugly, and when the two horses were fighting it out, neck and neck, up the back stretch, and when Tom was tooling Bucephalus smoothly and surely to the front, the older man turned in his sulky to glare at him. 'You damned little whipper-snapper,' he yelled, 'I'll knock you out of your sulky if you don't take back.'

He had yelled that at Tom, and then had struck at the boy with the butt of his whip – not intending actually to hit him, perhaps, but just missing the boy's head, and Tom had kept his eyes steadily on his own horse, had held him smoothly in his stride, and at the upper turn, at just the right moment, had begun to pull out in front.

Later, he hadn't even told Harry Whitehead of the incident, and that fact, too, he felt vaguely, had something to do with his qualifications as a man.

And now they were going to put him into a school with the kids. He was at work on the stable floor, rubbing the legs of a trim-looking colt, and Bucephalus was in his stall waiting to be taken to a late fall meeting at Indianapolis on the following Monday, when the blow fell. Harry Whitehead walked back and forth, swearing at the two men who were loafing in chairs at the stable door. 'Do you call that law, eh, robbing a kid of the chance Tom's got?' he asked, shaking a riding-whip under their noses. 'I never see such a law. What I say is, Dod blast such a law.'

Tom took the colt back to its place and went into Bucephalus' box-stall. The stallion was in one of his gentle moods and turned to have his nose rubbed, but Tom went and buried his face against the great black neck and for a long time stood thus, trembling. He had thought perhaps Harry would let him drive Bucephalus in all his races another season, and now that was all to come to an end and he was to be pitched back into childhood, to be made just a kid in school. 'I won't do it,' he decided suddenly, and a dogged light came into his eyes. His future as a driver of race-horses might have to be sacrificed, but that didn't matter so much as the humiliation of this other, and he decided he would say nothing to Harry Whitehead or his wife, but would make his own move.

'I'll get out of here. Before they get me into that school I'll skip out of town,' he told himself as his hand crept up and fondled the soft nose of Bucephalus, the son royal of the Patchens.

Tom left Bidwell during the night, going east on a freight train, and no one there ever saw him again. During that winter he lived in the city of Cleveland, where he got work driving a milk-wagon in a district where factory workers lived.

Then spring came again, and with it the memory of other springs – of thunder-showers rolling over fields of wheat, just appearing, green and vivid, out of the black ground – of the sweet smell of new ploughed fields, and most of all the smell and sound of animals about barns at the Whitehead farms north of Bidwell. How sharply he remembered those days on the farms and the days later, when he lived in Bidwell, slept in the stables, and went each morning to jog race-horses and young colts round and round the half-mile race-track at the fair-grounds at Bidwell.

That was a life! Round and round the track they went, young colthood and young manhood together, not thinking, but carrying life very keenly within themselves and feeling tremendously. The colts' legs were to be hardened and their wind made sound, and for the boy long hours were to be spent in a kind of dream world, and life lived in the company of something fine, courageous, filled with a terrible, waiting surge of life. At the fair-ground, away at the town's edge, tall grass grew in the enclosure inside the track, and there were trees from which came the voices of squirrels, chattering and scolding, accompanied by the call of nesting birds and, down below on the ground, by the song of bees visiting early blossoms and of insects hidden away in the grass.

How different the life of the city streets in the spring-time! To Tom it was in a way fetid and foul. For months he had been living in a boarding-house with some six, and often eight or ten, other young fellows, in narrow rooms above a foul street. The young fellows were un-married and made good wages, and on the winter evenings and on Sundays they dressed in good clothes and went forth, to return later, half-drunk, to sit for long hours boasting and talking loudly in the rooms. Because he was shy, often lonely, and sometimes startled and frightened by what he saw and heard in the city, the others would have nothing to do with Tom. They felt a kind of contempt for him, looked upon him as a 'rube,' and in the late afternoon when his work was done he often went for long walks alone in grim streets of working-men's houses, breathing the smoke-laden air and listening to the roar and clatter of machinery in great factories. At other times, and immediately after the evening meal, he went off to his room and to bed, half-sick with fear and with some strange nameless dread of the life about him.

And so in the early summer of his seventeenth year Tom left the city and, going back into his own Northern Ohio lake country, found work with a man named John Bottsford, who owned a threshing outfit and worked among the farmers of Erie County, Ohio. The slender boy, who had urged Bucephalus to his greatest victory and had driven him the fastest mile of his career, had become a tall, strong fellow with heavy features, brown eyes, and big nerveless hands — but in spite of his apparent heaviness there was something tremendously alive in him. He now drove a team of plodding grey farm-horses, and it was his job to keep the threshing engine supplied with water and fuel and to haul the threshed grain out of the fields and into farmers' barns.

The thresherman Bottsford was a broad-shouldered, powerful old man of sixty and had, besides Tom, three grown sons in his employ. He had been a farmer, working on rented land, all his life and had saved some money, with which he had bought the threshing outfit, and all day the five men worked like driven slaves and at night slept in the hay in the farmers' barns. It was rainy that

season in the lake country, and at the beginning of the time
of threshing things did not go very well for Bottsford.

The old thresherman was worried. The threshing
venture had taken all of his money and he had a dread of
going into debt, and, as he was a deeply religious man, at
night, when he thought the others asleep, he crawled out
of the hay-loft and went down on to the barn floor to
pray.

Something happened to Tom, and for the first time in
his life he began to think about life and its meaning. He
was in the country that he loved, in the yellow sun-
washed fields, far from the dreaded noises and dirt of city
life, and here was a man, of his own type, in some deep
way a brother to himself, who was continuously crying
out to some power outside himself, some power that was in
the sun, in the clouds, in the roaring thunder that accompanied the summer rains – that was in these things and
that at the same time controlled all these things.

The young threshing apprentice was impressed.
Throughout the rainy days, when no work could be done,
he wandered about and waited for night, and then, when
they all had gone into the barn loft and the others prepared
to sleep, he stayed awake to think and listen. He thought
of God and of the possibilities of God's part in the affairs
of men. The thresherman's youngest son, a fat, jolly
fellow, lay beside him, and for a time after they had crawled
into the hay the two boys whispered and laughed together. The fat boy's skin was sensitive and the dry broken
ends of grass stalks crept down under his clothes and
tickled him. He giggled and twisted about, wriggling and
kicking, and Tom looked at him and laughed also. The
thoughts of God went out of his mind.

In the barn all became quiet, and when it rained a low drumming sound went on overhead. Tom could hear the horses and cattle, down below, moving about. The smells were all delicious smells. The smell of the cows in particular awoke something heady in him. It was as though he had been drinking strong wine. Every part of his body seemed alive. The two older boys, who, like their father, had serious natures, lay with their feet buried in the hay. They lay very still and a warm musty smell arose from their clothes, that were full of the sweat of toil. Presently the bearded old thresherman, who slept off by himself, arose cautiously and walked across the hay in his stockinged feet. He went down a ladder to the floor below, and Tom listened eagerly. The fat boy snored, but he was quite sure that the older boys were awake like himself. Every sound from below was magnified. He heard a horse stamp on the barn floor and a cow rub her horns against a feed-box. The old thresherman prayed fervently, calling on the name of Jesus to help him out of his difficulty. Tom could not hear all his words, but some of them came to him quite clearly, and one group of words ran like a refrain through the thresherman's prayer. 'Gentle Jesus,' he cried, 'send the good days. Let the good days come quickly. Look out over the land. Send us the fair warm days.'

Came the warm fair days and Tom wondered. Late every morning, after the sun had marched far up into the sky and after the machines were set by a great pile of wheat bundles, he drove his tank-wagon off to be filled at some distant creek or at a pond. Sometimes he was compelled to drive two or three miles to the lake. Dust gathered in the roads and the horses plodded along. He passed through a grove of trees and went down a lane and into a small valley where there was a spring, and he thought of the old man's words, uttered in the silence and the darkness of the barns. He made himself a figure of Jesus as a young god walking about over the land. The young god went through the lanes and through the shaded covered places. The feet of the horses came down with a thump in the dust of the road and there was an echoing thump far away in the wood. Tom leaned forward and listened and his cheeks became a little pale. He was no longer the growing man, but had become again the fine and sensitive boy who had driven Bucephalus through a mob of angry, determined men to victory. For the first time the blood of the old poet Twn O'r Nant awoke in him.

The water boy for the threshing crew rode the horse Pegasus down through the lanes back of the farm-houses in Erie County, Ohio, to the creeks where the threshing tanks must be filled. Beside him on the soft earth in the forest walked the young god Jesus. At the creek Pegasus, born of the springs of Ocean, stamped on the ground. The plodding farm-horses stopped. With a dazed look in his eyes Tom Edwards arose from the wagon seat and prepared his hose and pump for filling the tank. The god Jesus walked away over the land, and with a wave of his hand summoned the smiling days.

A light came into Tom Edwards' eyes and grace seemed to come also into his heavy maturing body. New impulses came to him. As the threshing crew went about, over the roads and through the villages from farm to farm, women and young girls looked at the young man and smiled. Sometimes as he came from the fields to a farmer's barn, with a load of wheat in bags on his wagon, the daughter of the farmer stepped out of the farm-house and stood looking at him. Tom looked at the woman and hunger crept into his heart, and in the evenings, while the thresherman and his sons sat on the ground by the barns and talked of their affairs, he walked nervously about. Making a motion to the fat boy, who was not really interested in the talk of his father and brothers, the two younger men went to walk in the nearby fields and on the roads. Sometimes they stumbled along a country road in the dusk of the evening and came into the lighted streets of a town. Under the store-lights young girls walked about. The two boys stood in the shadows by a building and watched, and later, as they went homeward in the darkness, the fat boy expressed what they both felt. They passed through a dark place where the road wound through a wood. In silence the frogs croaked, and birds roosting in the trees were disturbed by their presence and fluttered about. The fat boy wore heavy overalls and his fat legs rubbed against each other. The rough cloth made a queer creaking sound. He spoke passionately. 'I would like to hold a woman, tight, tight, tight,' he said.

One Sunday the thresherman took his entire crew with him to a church. They had been working near a village called Castalia, but did not go into the town, but to a small white frame church that stood amid trees and by a stream at the side of a road, a mile north of the village. They went on Tom's water-wagon, from which they had lifted the tank and placed boards for seats. The boy drove the horses.

Many teams were tied in the shade under the trees in a little grove near the church, and strange men — farmers and their sons — stood about in little groups and talked of the season's crops. Although it was hot, a breeze played among the leaves of the trees under which they stood, and back of the church and the grove the stream ran over stones and made a persistent, soft, murmuring noise that arose above the hum of voices.

In the church Tom sat beside the fat boy, who stared at the country girls as they came in and who, after the sermon began, went to sleep, while Tom listened eagerly to the sermon. The minister, an old man with a beard and a strong sturdy body, looked, he thought, not unlike his employer, Bottsford the thresherman.

The minister in the country church talked of that time when Mary Magdalene, the woman who had been taken in adultery, was being stoned by the crowd of men who had forgotten their own sins, and when, in the tale the minister told, Jesus approached and rescued the woman Tom's heart thumped with excitement. Then later, the minister talked of how Jesus was tempted by the Devil as He stood on a high place in the mountain, but the boy did not listen. He leaned forward and looked out through a window across fields and the minister's words came to him but in broken sentences. Tom took what was said concerning the temptations on the mountain to mean that Mary had followed Jesus and had offered her body to Him, and that afternoon, when he had returned with the others to the farm where they were to begin threshing on the next morning, he called the fat boy aside and asked his opinion.

The two boys walked across a field of wheat-stubble and sat down on a log in a grove of trees. It had never occurred to Tom that a man could be tempted by a woman. It had always seemed to him that it must be the other way, that women must always be tempted by men. 'I thought men always asked,' he said, 'and now it seems that women sometimes do the asking. That would be a fine thing if it could happen to us. Don't you think so?'

The two boys arose and walked under the trees and dark shadows began to form on the ground underfoot. Tom burst into words and continually asked questions, and the fat boy, who had been often to church, and for whom the figure of Jesus had lost most of its reality, felt a little embarrassed. He did not think the subject should be thus freely discussed and when Tom's mind kept playing with the notion of Jesus pursued and tempted by a woman, he grunted his disapproval. 'Do you think He really refused?' Tom asked over and over. The fat boy tried to explain. 'He had twelve disciples,' he said. 'It couldn't have happened. They were always about. Well, you see, she wouldn't ever have had no chance. Wherever He went they went with Him. They were men He was teaching to preach. One of them later betrayed Him to soldiers who killed Him.'

Tom wondered. 'How did that come about? How could a man like that be betrayed?' he asked. 'By a kiss,' the fat boy replied.

On the evening of the day when Tom Edwards – for the first and last time in his life – went into a church there was a light shower, the only one that fell upon John Bottsford's threshing crew during the last three months the Welsh boy was with them, and the shower in no way interfered with their work. The shower came up suddenly and in a few minutes was gone. As it was Sunday, and as there was no work, the men had all gathered in the barn and were looking out through the open barn doors. Two or three men from the farm-house came and sat with them on boxes and barrels on the barn floor and, as is customary

with country people, very little was said. The men took
knives out of their pockets and, finding little sticks among
the rubbish on the barn floor, began to whittle, while the
old thresherman went restlessly about with his hands in his
trouser pockets. Tom, who sat near the door, where an
occasional drop of rain was blown against his cheek, alter-
nately looked from his employer to the open country
where the rain played over the fields. One of the farmers
remarked that a rainy time had come on and that there
would be no good threshing weather for several days, and,
while the thresherman did not answer, Tom saw his lips
move and his grey beard bob up and down. He thought
the thresherman was protesting, but did not want to protest
in words.

As they had gone about the country many rains had
passed to the north, south and east of the threshing crew,
and on some days the clouds hung over them all day, but
no rain fell, and when they had got to a new place they
were told it had rained there three days before. Sometimes when they left a farm Tom stood up on the seat of
his water-wagon and looked back. He looked across fields
to where they had been at work and then looked up into
the sky. 'The rain may come now. The threshing is
done and the wheat is all in the barn. The rain can now do
no harm to our labour,' he thought.

On the Sunday evening when he sat with the men on
the floor of the barn Tom was sure that the shower that
had now come would be but a passing affair. He thought
his employer must be very close to Jesus, who controlled
the affairs of the heavens, and that a long rain would not
come because the thresherman did not want it. He fell
into a deep reverie and John Bottsford came and stood

close beside him. The thresherman put his hand against the door-jamb and looked out, and Tom could still see the grey beard moving. The man was praying and was so close to himself that his trouser-leg touched Tom's hand. Into the boy's mind came the remembrance of how John Bottsford had prayed at night on the barn floor. On that very morning he had prayed. It was just as daylight came, and the boy was awakened because, as he crept across the hay to descend the ladder, the old man's foot had touched his hand.

As always, Tom had been excited and wanted to hear every word said in the older man's prayers. He lay tense, listening to every sound that came up from below. A faint glow of light came into the hay-loft through a crack in the side of the barn, a rooster crowed, and some pigs, housed in a pen near the barn, grunted loudly. They had heard the thresherman moving about and wanted to be fed, and their grunting, and the occasional restless movement of a horse or a cow in the stable below, prevented Tom's hearing very distinctly. He, however, made out that his employer was thanking Jesus for the fine weather that had attended them, and was protesting that he did not want to be selfish in asking it to continue. 'Jesus,' he said, 'send, if you wish, a little shower on this day when, because of our love for you, we do not work in the fields. Let it be fine to-morrow, but to-day, after we have come back from the house of worship, let a shower freshen the land.'

As Tom sat on a box near the door of the barn and saw how aptly the words of his employer had been answered by Jesus, he knew that the rain would not last. The man for whom he worked seemed to him so close to the throne of God that he raised the hand that had been touched by

John Bottsford's trouser-leg to his lips and secretly kissed it – and when he looked again out over the fields the clouds were being blown away by a wind and the evening sun was coming out. It seemed to him that the young and beautiful god Jesus must be right at hand, within hearing of his voice. 'He is,' Tom told himself, 'standing behind a tree in the orchard.' The rain stopped and he went silently out of the barn, towards a small apple orchard that lay beside the farm-house, but when he came to a fence and was about to climb over, he stopped. 'If Jesus is there He will not want me to find Him,' he thought. As he turned again toward the barn, he could see, across a field, a low grass-covered hill. He decided that Jesus was not, after all, in the orchard. The long slanting rays of the evening sun fell on the crest of the hill and touched with light the grass stalks, heavy with drops of rain, and for a moment the hill was crowned as with a crown of jewels. A million tiny drops of water, reflecting the light, made the hill-top sparkle as though set with gems. 'Jesus is there,. muttered the boy. 'He lies on His belly in the grass. He is looking at me over the edge of the hill.'

CHAPTER II

JOHN BOTTSFORD went with his threshing crew to work for a large farmer named Barton, near the town of Sandusky. The threshing season was drawing near an end and the days remained clear, cool and beautiful. The country into which he now came made a deep impression on Tom's mind and he never forgot the thoughts and experiences that came to him during the last weeks of that summer on the Barton farms.

The traction engine, puffing forth smoke and attracting the excited attention of dogs and children as it rumbled along and pulled the heavy red grain-separator, had trailed slowly over miles of road and had come down almost to Lake Erie. Tom, with the fat Bottsford boy sitting beside him on the water-wagon, followed the rumbling, puffing engine, and when they came to the new place, where they were to stay for several days, he could see, from the wagon seat, the smoke of the factories in the town of Sandusky rising into the clear morning air.

The man for whom John Bottsford was threshing owned three farms, one on an island in the bay, where he lived, and two on the mainland, and the larger of the mainland farms had great stacks of wheat standing in a field near the barns. The farm was in a wide basin of land, very fertile, through which a creek flowed northward into Sandusky Bay, and besides the stacks of wheat in the basin, other stacks had been made in the upland fields beyond the creek, where a country of low hills began. From these latter fields the waters of the bay could be seen glistening in the bright fall sunlight, and steamers went from Sandusky to a pleasure resort called Cedar Point. When the wind blew from the north or west, and when the threshing machinery had been stopped at the noon hour, the men, resting with their backs against a straw-stack, could hear a band playing on one of the steamers.

Fall came on early that year, and the leaves on the trees in the forests that grew along the roads that ran down through the low creek bottom lands began to turn yellow and red. In the afternoon when Tom went to the creek for water he walked beside his horses, and the dry leaves crackled and snapped underfoot.

As the season had been a prosperous one, Bottsford decided that his youngest son should attend school in town during the fall and winter. He had bought himself a machine for cutting firewood and, with his two older sons, intended to take up that work. 'The logs will have to be hauled out of the wood lots to where we set up the saws,' he said to Tom. 'You can come with us if you wish.'

The thresherman began to talk to Tom of the value of learning. 'You'd better go to some town yourself this winter. It would be better for you to get into a school,' he said sharply. He grew excited and walked up and down beside the water-wagon, on the seat of which Tom sat listening, and said that God had given men both minds and bodies and it was wicked to let either decay because of neglect. 'I have watched you,' he said. 'You don't talk very much, but you do plenty of thinking, I guess. Go into the schools. Find out what the books have to say. You don't have to believe when they say things that are lies.'

The Bottsford family lived in a rented house facing a stone road near the town of Bellevue, and the fat boy was to go to that town – a distance of some eighteen miles from where the men were at work – afoot, and on the evening before he set out he and Tom went out of the barns, intending to have a last walk and talk together on the roads.

They went along in the dusk of the fall evening, each thinking his own thoughts, and, coming to a bridge that led over the creek in the valley, sat on the bridge rail. Tom had little to say, but his companion wanted to talk about women, and, when darkness came on, the embarrassment he felt regarding the subject went quite away and he talked boldly and freely. He said that in the town of Belle-vue, where he was to live and attend school during the coming winter, he would be sure to get in with a woman. 'I'm not going to be cheated out of that chance,' he declared. He explained that, as his father would be away from home when he moved into town, he would be free to pick his own place to board.

The fat boy's imagination became inflamed and he told Tom his plans. 'I won't try to get in with any young girl,' he declared shrewdly. 'That only gets a fellow in a fix. He might have to marry her. I'll go live in a house with a widow, that's what I'll do. And in the evening the two of us will be there alone. We'll begin to talk and I'll keep touching her with my hands. That will get her excited.'

The fat boy jumped to his feet and walked back and forth on the bridge. He was nervous and a little ashamed, and wanted to justify what he had said. The thing for which he hungered had, he thought, become a possibility – an act half achieved. Coming to stand before Tom, he put a hand on his shoulder. 'I'll go into her room at night,' he declared. 'I'll not tell her I'm coming, but will creep in when she is asleep. Then I'll get down on my knees by her bed and I'll kiss her, hard, hard. I'll hold her tight, so she can't get away, and I'll kiss her mouth till she wants what I want. Then I'll stay in her house all winter. No one will know. Even if she won't have me, I'll only have to move; I'm sure to be safe. No one will believe what she says, if she tells on me. I'm not going to be like a boy any more. I'll tell you what – I'm as big as a man and I'm going to do like men do, that's what I am.'

The two young men went back to the barn where they were to sleep on the hay. The rich farmer for whom they were now at work had a large house and provided beds for the thresherman and his two older sons, but the two younger men slept in the barn loft, and on the night before had lain under one blanket. After the talk by the bridge, however, Tom did not feel very comfortable, and that stout exponent of manhood, the younger Bottsford, was also embarrassed. In the road the young man, whose name was Paul, walked a little ahead of his companion, and when they got to the barn each sought a separate place in the loft. Each wanted to have thoughts into which he did not want the presence of the other to intrude.

For the first time Tom's body burned with eager desire for a female. He lay where he could see out through a crack in the side of the barn, and at first his thoughts were all about animals. He had brought a horse-blanket up from the stable below and, crawling under it, lay on his side with his eyes close to the crack and thought about the love-making of horses and cattle. Things he had seen in the stables when he worked for Whitehead, the racing man, came back to his mind and a queer animal hunger ran through him, so that his legs stiffened. He rolled restlessly about on the hay and, for some reason he did not understand, his lust took the form of anger, and he hated the fat boy. He thought he would like to crawl over the hay and pound his companion's face with his fists. Although he had not seen Paul Bottsford's face when he talked of the widow, he had sensed in him a flavour of triumph. 'He thinks he has got the better of me,' young Edwards thought.

He rolled again to the crack and stared out into the night. There was a new moon and the fields were dimly outlined, and clumps of trees along the road that led into the town of Sandusky looked like black clouds that had settled down over the land. For some reason the sight of the land, lying dim and quiet under the moon, took all of his anger away and he began to think, not of Paul Bottsford, with hot eager lust in his eyes, creeping into the room of the widow at Bellevue, but of the god Jesus, going up into a mountain with his woman, Mary.

His companion's notion of going into a room where a woman lay sleeping and taking her, as it were, unawares now seemed to him entirely mean, and the hot jealous feeling that had turned into anger and hatred went entirely away. He tried to think what the god, who had brought the beautiful days for the threshing, would do with a woman.

Tom's body still burned with desire and his mind wanted to think lascivious thoughts. The moon that had been hidden behind clouds emerged and a wind began to blow. It was still early evening, and in the town of Sandusky pleasure-seekers were taking the boat to the resort over the bay, and the wind brought to Tom's ears the sound of music, blown over the waters of the bay and down the creek basin. In a grove near the barn the wind swayed gently the branches of young trees and black shadows ran here and there on the ground.

The younger Bottsford had gone to sleep in a distant part of the barn loft, and now began to snore loudly. The tenseness went out of Tom's legs and he prepared to sleep, but before sleeping he muttered, half timidly, certain words, that were half a prayer, half an appeal, to some spirit of the night. 'Jesus, bring me a woman,' he whispered.

Outside the barn, in the fields, the wind, becoming a little stronger, picked up bits of straw and blew them about

213

among the hard upstanding stubble, and there was a low, gentle, whispering sound as though the gods were answering his appeal.

Tom went to sleep with his arm under his head and with his eye close to the crack that gave him a view of the moonlit fields, and in his dream the cry from within repeated itself over and over. The mysterious god Jesus had heard and answered the needs of his employer, John Bottsford, and his own need would, he was quite sure, be understood and attended to. 'Bring me a woman. I need her. Jesus, bring me a woman,' he kept whispering into the night, as consciousness left him and he slipped away into dreams.

After the youngest of the Bottsfords had departed a change took place in the nature of Tom's work. The threshing crew had got now into a country of large farms where the wheat had all been brought in from the fields and stacked near the barns, and where there was always plenty of water near at hand. Everything was simplified. The separator was pulled in close by the barn door and the threshed grain was carried directly to the bins from the separator. As it was not a part of Tom's work to feed the bundles of grain into the whirling teeth of the separator – this work being done by John Bottsford's two elder sons – there was little for the crew's teamster to do. Sometimes John Bottsford, who was the engineer, departed, going to make arrangements for the next stop, and was gone for a half-day, and at such times Tom, who had picked up some knowledge of the art, ran the engine.

On other days, however, there was nothing at all for him to do, and his mind, unoccupied for long hours, began to play him tricks. In the morning, after his team had been fed and cleaned until the grey coats of the old farm-horses shone like racers, he went out of the barn and into an orchard. Filling his pockets with ripe apples, he went to a fence and leaned over. In a field young colts played about. As he held the apples and called softly they came timidly forward, stopping in alarm and then running a little forward, until one of them, bolder than the others, ate one of the apples out of his hand.

All through those bright, warm, clear fall days a restless feeling, it seemed to Tom, ran through everything in nature. In the clumps of woodland still standing on the farms flaming red spread itself out along the limbs of trees, and there was one grove of young maple trees, near a barn, that was like a troop of girls, young girls who had walked together down a sloping field, to stop in alarm at seeing the men at work in the barn-yard. Tom stood looking at the trees. A slight breeze made them sway gently from side to side. Two horses standing among the trees drew near each other. One nipped the other's neck. They rubbed their heads together.

The crew stopped at another large farm, and it was to be their last stop for the season. 'When we have finished this job we'll go home and get our own fall-work done,' Bottsford said. Saturday evening came, and the thresherman and his sons took the horses and drove away, going to their own home for the Sunday, and leaving Tom alone. 'We'll be back early on Monday morning,' the thresherman said as they drove away. Sunday alone among the strange farm people brought a sharp experience to Tom, and when it had passed he decided he would not wait for the end of the threshing season – but a few days off now but would quit his job and go into the city and surrender to the schools. He remembered his employer's words: 'Find out what the books have to say. You don't have to believe when they say things that are lies.'

As he walked in lanes, across meadows, and upon the hill-sides of the farm, also on the shores of Sandusky Bay, that Sunday morning Tom thought almost constantly of his friend the fat fellow, young Paul Bottsford, who had gone to spend the fall and winter at Bellevue, and wondered what his life there might be like. He had himself lived in such a town, in Bidwell, but had rarely left Harry White-head's stable. What went on in such a town? What happened at night in the houses of the towns? He remembered Paul's plan for getting into a house alone with a widow, and how he was to creep into her room at night, holding her tightly in his arms until she wanted what he wanted. 'I wonder if he will have the nerve. Gee, I wonder if he will have the nerve,' he muttered.

For a long time, ever since Paul had gone away and he had no one with whom he could talk, things had taken on a new aspect in Tom's mind. The rustle of dry leaves underfoot, as he walked in a forest, the playing of shadows over the open face of a field, the murmuring song of insects in the dry grass beside the fences in the lanes – and at night the hushed contented sounds made by the animals in the barns, were no longer so sweet to him. For him, no more did the young god Jesus walk beside him, just out of sight behind low hills, or down the dry beds of streams. Something within himself that had been sleeping was now awakening. When he returned from walking in the fields on the fall evenings and, thinking of Paul Bottsford alone in the house with the widow at Bellevue, half wishing he were in the same position, he felt ashamed in the presence of the gentle old thresherman, and afterwards did not lie awake listening to the older man's prayers. The men who had come from nearby farms to help with the threshing laughed and shouted to each other as they pitched the straw into great stacks or carried the filled bags of grain to the bins, and they had wives and daughters who had come with them, and who were now at work in the farm-house kitchen, from which also laughter came. Girls and women kept coming out at the kitchen door into the barn-yard, tall, awkward girls, plump, red-cheeked girls, women with worn, thin faces and sagging breasts. All men and women seemed made for each other.

They all laughed and talked together, understood one another. Only he was alone. He only had no one to whom he could feel warm and close, to whom he could draw close.

On the Sunday when the Bottsfords had all gone away, Tom came in from walking all morning in the fields and ate his dinner with many other people in a big farm-house dining-room. In preparation for the threshing days ahead, and the feeding of many people, several women had come to spend the day and to help in preparing food. The farmer's daughter, who was married and lived in Sandusky, came with her husband, and three other women, neighbours, came from farms in the neighbourhood. Tom did not look at them, but ate his dinner in silence, and as soon as he could manage got out of the house and went to the barns. Going into a long shed, he sat on the tongue of a wagon that from long disuse was covered with dust. Swallows flew back and forth among the rafters overhead and, in an upper corner of the shed where they evidently had a nest, wasps buzzed in the semi-darkness.

The daughter of the farmer, who had come from town, came from the house with a babe in her arms. It was nursing time, and she wanted to escape from the crowded house, and, without having seen Tom, she sat on a box near the shed door and opened her dress. Embarrassed and at the same time fascinated by the sight of a woman's breasts, seen through cracks of the wagon-box, Tom drew his legs up and his head down and remained concealed until the woman had gone back to the house. Then he went again to the fields and did not go back to the house for the evening meal.

As he walked on that Sunday afternoon the grandson of the Welsh poet experienced many new sensations. In a way he came to understand that the things Paul had talked of doing and that had, but a short time before, filled him with disgust were now possible to himself also. In the past, when he had thought about women, there had always been something healthy and animal-like in his lusts, but now they took a new form. The passion that could not find expression through his body went up into his mind, and he began to see visions. Women became to him something different than anything else in nature, more desirable than anything else in nature, and at the same time everything in nature became woman. The trees in the apple orchard by the barn were like the arms of women. The apples on the trees were round like the breasts of women. They were the breasts of women – and when he had got on to a low hill the contour of the fences that marked the confines of the fields fell into the forms of women's bodies. Even the clouds in the sky did the same thing.

He walked down along a lane to a stream and crossed the stream by a wooden bridge. Then he climbed another hill, the highest place in all that part of the country, and there the fever that possessed him became more active. An odd lassitude crept over him and he lay down in the grass on the hill-top and closed his eyes. For a long time he remained in a hushed, half-sleeping, dreamless state, and then opened his eyes again.

Again the forms of women floated before him. To his left the bay was ruffled by a gentle breeze, and far over toward the city of Sandusky two sail-boats were apparently engaged in a race. The masts of the boats were fully dressed, but on the great stretch of water they seemed to stand still. The bay itself, in Tom's eyes, had taken on the form and shape of a woman's head and body, and the two sail-boats were the woman's eyes looking at him.

The bay was a woman with her head lying where lay the city of Sandusky. Smoke arose from the stacks of steamers docked at the city's wharves, and the smoke formed itself into masses of black hair. Through the farm where he had come to thresh ran a stream. It swept down past the foot of the hill on which he lay. The stream was the arm of the woman. Her hand was thrust into the land and the lower part of her body was lost – far down to the north, where the bay became a part of Lake Erie – but her other arm could be seen. It was outlined in the farther shore of the bay. Her other arm was drawn up and her hand was pressing against her face. Her form was distorted by pain, but at the same time the giant woman smiled at the boy on the hill. There was something in the smile that was like the smile that had come unconsciously to the lips of the woman who had nursed her child in the shed.

Turning his face away from the bay, Tom looked at the

sky. A great white cloud that lay along the southern horizon formed itself into the giant head of a man. Tom watched as the cloud crept slowly across the sky. There was something noble and quieting about the giant's face, and his hair, pure white and as thick as wheat in a rich field in June, added to its nobility. Only the face appeared. Below the shoulders there was just a white shapeless mass of clouds.

And then this formless mass began also to change. The face of a giant woman appeared. It pressed upward toward the face of the man. Two arms formed themselves on the man's shoulders and pressed the woman closely. The two faces merged. Something seemed to snap in Tom's brain.

He sat upright and looked neither at the bay nor at the sky. Evening was coming on and soft shadows began to play over the land. Below him lay the farm with its barns and houses, and in the field, below the hill on which he was lying, there were two smaller hills that became at once in his eyes the two full breasts of a woman. Two white sheep appeared and stood nibbling the grass on the woman's breasts. They were like babes being suckled. The trees in the orchards near the barns were the woman's hair. An arm of the stream that ran down to the bay, the stream he had crossed on the wooden bridge when he came to the hill, cut across a meadow beyond the two low hills. It widened into a pond, and the pond made a mouth for the woman. Her eyes were two black hollows – low spots in a field where hogs had routed the grass away, looking for roots. Black puddles of water lay in the hollows and they seemed eyes shining invitingly up at him.

This woman also smiled, and her smile was now an invitation. Tom got to his feet and hurried away down the hill and, going stealthily past the barns and the house, got into a road. All night he walked under the stars, thinking new thoughts. 'I am obsessed with this idea of having a woman. I'd better go to the city and go to school, and see if I can make myself fit to have a woman of my own,' he thought. 'I won't sleep to-night but will wait until to-morrow, when Bottsford comes back, and then I'll quit and go into the city.' He walked, trying to make plans. Even a good man like John Bottsford had a woman for himself. Could he do that?

The thought was exciting. At the moment it seemed to him that he had only to go into the city, and go to the schools for a time, to become beautiful and to have beautiful women love him. In his half-ecstatic state he forgot the winter months he had spent in the city of Cleveland, and forgot also the grim streets, the long rows of dark prison-like factories, and the loneliness of his life in the city. For the moment, and as he walked in the dusty roads under the moon, he thought of American towns and cities as places for beautifully satisfying adventures for all such fellows as himself.

PRINTED BY BUTLER AND TANNER LTD., FROME AND LONDON.

A LIST OF VOLUMES ISSUED IN
THE TRAVELLERS' LIBRARY

$1·00 each

NEW YORK

JONATHAN CAPE & HARRISON SMITH

139 EAST FORTY-SIXTH STREET

A series of books in all branches of literature designed for the pocket, or for the small house where shelf space is scarce. Though the volumes measure only 7 inches by 4¾ inches, the page is arranged so that the margins are not unreasonably curtailed nor legibility sacrificed. The books are of a uniform thickness irrespective of the number of pages, and the paper, specially manufactured for the series, is remarkably opaque, even when it is thinnest.

A semi-flexible form of binding has been adopted, as a safeguard against the damage inevitably associated with hasty packing. The cloth is of a particularly attractive shade of blue and has the author's name stamped in gold on the back.

ANDERSON, Sherwood (54)
HORSES AND MEN

¶ 'It has a unity beyond that of its constant Middle-west setting. A man of poetic vision, with an intimate knowledge of particular conditions of life, here looks out upon a world that seems singularly material only because he unflinchingly accepts its actualities.' *Morning Post*

BUTLER, Samuel (55)
SELECTED ESSAYS

¶ This volume contains the following essays:

The Humour of Homer	How to Make the Best of Life
Quis Desiderio . . .?	The Sanctuary of Montrigone
Ramblings in Cheapside	A Medieval Girls' School
The Aunt, the Nieces and the Dog	Art in the Valley of Saas
	Thought and Language

COPPARD, A. E. (2)
THE BLACK DOG. A volume of Stories

¶ 'Mr. Coppard is a born story-teller. The book is filled with a variety of delightful stuff: no one who is interested in good writing in general, and good short stories in particular, should miss it.' *Spectator*

DAVIES, W. H. (3)

THE AUTOBIOGRAPHY OF A SUPER-TRAMP
With a preface by G. BERNARD SHAW

¶ Printed as it was written, it is worth reading for its literary style alone. The author tells us with inimitable quiet modesty of how he begged and stole his way across America and through England and Wales until his travelling days were cut short by losing his right foot while attempting to 'jump' a train.

DAVIES, W. H. (48)

LATER DAYS
A pendant to *The Autobiography of a Super-Tramp*

¶ 'The self-portrait is given with disarming, mysterious, and baffling directness, and the writing has the same disarmingness and simpleness.' *Observer*

DAVIES, W. H. (56)

A POET'S PILGRIMAGE

¶ *A Poet's Pilgrimage* recounts the author's impressions of his native Wales on his return after many years' absence. He tells of a walking tour during which he stayed in cheap rooms and ate in the small wayside inns. The result is a vivid picture of the Welsh people, the towns and countryside.

HILDEBRAND, Arthur Sturges (36)

BLUE WATER

¶ This book gives the real feeling of life on a small cruising yacht; the nights on deck with the sails against the sky, long fights with head winds by mountainous coasts to safety in forlorn little island ports, and constant adventure free from care.

HUDDLESTON, Sisley (86)

FRANCE AND THE FRENCH

¶ 'There has been nothing of its kind published since the War. His book is a repository of facts marshalled with judgment; as such it should assist in clearing away a whole maze of misconceptions and prejudices, and serve as a sort of pocket encyclopædia of modern France.' *Times Literary Supplement*

KALLAS, AINO (24)
THE WHITE SHIP. STORIES
With an Introduction by JOHN GALSWORTHY

¶ 'The writer has an extraordinary sense of atmosphere.'
Times Literary Supplement
'Stories told convincingly and well, with a keen perception for
natural beauty.' *Nation*

LAWRENCE, D. H. (19)
TWILIGHT IN ITALY

¶ This volume of travel vignettes in North Italy was first published
in 1916. Since then Mr. Lawrence has increased the number
of his admirers year by year. In *Twilight in Italy* they will find
all the freshness and vigour of outlook which they have come to
expect from its author.

LUBBOCK, Percy (5)
THE CRAFT OF FICTION

¶ 'No more substantial or more charming volume of criticism has
been published in our time. *Observer*
'To say that this is the best book on the subject is probably true;
but it is more to the point to say that it is the only one.' *Times
Literary Supplement*

LUBBOCK, Percy (6)
EARLHAM

¶ 'The book seems too intimate to be reviewed. We want to be
allowed to read it, and to dream over it, and keep silence about
it. His judgment is perfect, his humour is true and ready; his
touch light and prim; his prose is exact and clean and full of
music.' *Times*

LUBBOCK, Percy (21)
ROMAN PICTURES

¶ Pictures of life as it is lived—or has been or might be lived—
among the pilgrims and colonists in Rome of more or less English
speech.
'A book of whimsical originality and exquisite workmanship,
and worthy of one of the best prose writers of our time.'
Sunday Times

MASON, Arthur (47)
THE FLYING BO'SUN

¶ 'What makes the book remarkable is the imaginative power which has re-created these events so vividly that even the super-natural ones come with the shock and the conviction with which actual supernatural events might come.' *From the Introduction by* EDWIN MUIR

MASON, Arthur (7)
WIDE SEAS AND MANY LANDS. A Personal Narrative
With an Introduction by MAURICE BARING

¶ 'This is an extremely entertaining, and at the same time, moving book. We are in the presence of a born writer. We read with the same mixture of amazement and delight that fills us through-out a Conrad novel.' *New Statesman*

MAUPASSANT, DE (37)
STORIES FROM, Translated by ELIZABETH MARTINDALE

¶ 'His "story" engrosses the non-critical, it holds the critical too at the first reading. . . . That is the real test of art, and it is because of the inobtrusiveness of this workmanship, that for once the critic and the reader may join hands without awaiting the verdict of posterity.' *From the Introduction by* FORD MADOX FORD

MITCHISON, Naomi (46)
WHEN THE BOUGH BREAKS
Stories of the time when Rome was crumbling to ruin

¶ 'Interesting, delightful, and fresh as morning dew. The connoisseur in short stories will turn to some pages in this volume again and again with renewed relish.' *Times Literary Supplement*

MURRAY, Max (61)
THE WORLD'S BACK DOORS
With an Introduction by HECTOR BOLITHO

¶ This book is not an account so much of places as of people. The journey round the world was begun with about enough money to buy one meal, and continued for 66,000 miles. There are periods as a longshore man and as a sailor, and a Chinese guard and a night watchman, and as a hobo.

O'FLAHERTY, Liam (26)
SPRING SOWING. STORIES

¶ 'Nothing seems to escape Mr. O'Flaherty's eye; his brain turns all things to drama; and his vocabulary is like a river in spate. *Spring Sowing* is a book to buy, or to borrow, or, yes, to steal.'
Bookman

RUTHERFORD, Mark (69)
THE REVOLUTION IN TANNER'S LANE

¶ 'Since Bunyan, English Puritanism has produced one imaginative genius of the highest order. To my mind, our fiction contains no more perfectly drawn pictures of English life in its recurring emotional contrast of excitement and repose more valuable to the historian, or more stimulating to the imaginative reader.' *H. W. Massingham*

RUTHERFORD, Mark (68)
THE DELIVERANCE OF MARK RUTHERFORD

¶ Once read, Hale White [Mark Rutherford] is never forgotten. But he is not yet approached through the highways of English letters. To the lover of his work, nothing can be more attractive than the pure and serene atmosphere of thought in which his art moves.

RUTHERFORD, Mark (67)
THE AUTOBIOGRAPHY OF MARK RUTHERFORD
With an introduction by H. W. MASSINGHAM

¶ Because of its honesty, delicacy and simplicity of portraiture, this book has always had a curious grip upon the affections of its readers. An English Amiel, inheriting to his comfort an English Old Crome landscape, he freed and strengthened his own spirit as he will his reader's.

THOMAS, Edward (97). Compiled by
THE POCKET BOOK OF POEMS AND SONGS FOR THE OPEN AIR

¶ This anthology is meant to please those lovers of poetry and the country who like a book that can always lighten some of their burdens or give wings to their delight, whether in the open air by day, or under the roof at evening; in it is gathered much of the finest English poetry.